Jeet Lo Marathon (Win Marathon)

Be a Hero

Aryan

Invincible Publishers

First published in India in 2017 by Invincible Publishers

ISBN: 978-93-87328-01-3

Invincible Publishers

G-120, Sushant Lok III, Sector 57, Gurugram-122002

Opposite Kasturba Ashram, Radaur Distt. Yamuna Nagar
Haryana-135133

Acknowledgement

To

The Universe

My Twin Flame

My Parents, who brought me into this world

My Brother, for always being with me

U.P. Sainik School, Lucknow

Dr. Wayne W Dyer

Paulo Coelho

Sandeep Maheshwari

Osho

Shiv Khera

People of the World

I Love You all!

“Be like a Diamond
Precious and Rare,
Not like a stone found
Everywhere.”

- Anonymous

The movie Jeet Lo Marathon is based on this book and has received a SEMI FINALIST CERTIFICATE at the Kyiv Film Festival, Ukraine as well as a World Premiere at the Cannes Film Market (Cannes Film Festival, 2017). The film is circuiting various International Festivals before it releases in India.

Contents

Introduction

Aryan is an ex-cadet of U.P. Sainik School. After wasting three years in Graduation, two years in Post-Graduation, two years in PG Diploma in International Business, two years in a Banking and Finance course and one year in an Insurance Facilitator certificate course, he decided to exit after having enrolled himself for a Ph.D. in Credit Risk Management from Kanpur University.

Aryan is still wasting his knowledge and experience in a Banking career and has been investing all his free time in writing this book, while simultaneously completing a film based on the same. His aim is to become completely time free. Purchase this book to help him realize his dream.

CHAPTER 1
PRESENT DAY

It was a usual morning. The sky was blue and the waves crashed loudly against the shore. Raj came running towards a high feature constructed just beyond the shore line, which was used decades ago for the purpose of drainage. Raj wore his favorite track-suit, representing the Indian Sports Team. A track-suit however, was not quite usual for Raj as he preferred sober gentle manly apparel which mostly included formal trousers, monotone shirts and formal black shoes paired with a sleek leather belt which helped him push his slight paunch inward.

Raj had been taking his usual practice runs and decided to go to the seaside that morning to rest. Or perhaps, there was something more on his mind that made him ponder.

Raj stood over the drainage structure, originally made by the British during their rule to cast out the garbage of the city. A huge pipe with a gaping mouth, jutting out of the mainland, chiefly composed the edifice, through which all the waste generated in the city of Mumbai got dumped into the sea. This structure remained above the water-level for only three hours during the low tide.

Raj climbed to the top of the historical construction and lost himself to the sight of the vast Arabian Sea, spread as far as his eyes could see, becoming one with the sky at the horizon. His hand reached for his pocket to take out a letter and holding it steadily, he unfolded it. The ends of the paper fluttered and flapped vigorously in his hands as the morning sea wind threatened to steal it away from him. The letter was from the Comrades Marathon Office in South Africa. He had been invited to participate in the prestigious Comrades Marathon. Raj couldn't contain himself as his eyes welled up and tears started rolling down his cheeks. He returned his gaze to the horizon and memories from recent past diffused through his mind, as if it were the present.

CHAPTER 2
MANASI, I LOVE YOU

Not much time had passed since Raj got married to the beautiful Manasi in the city of Nawabs, Lucknow. Like most Indian marriages, it was arranged by their respective families. Nothing better could have happened for the simple and down-to-earth Raj. Institutions like arranged marriage, where in fact designed for people like Raj who couldn't dare to approach a woman, even if they were in love. Raj drew a good salary from a private firm, which ranked his profile high on matrimonial websites. Manasi, despite being an ambitious girl, hadn't had the opportunity to pursue her career since she belonged to the city of Kanpur where young men couldn't travel on bikes or scooters with their sisters, for the fear of being misunderstood as lovers and getting beaten down to earth before they could utter so much as a word. Manasi was like a dream trapped in the cage of reality. All of Manasi's life decisions were taken by her mother and father, with no regard to her opinion whatsoever.

It was at their wedding night, that Manasi got to know Raj for the first time. She couldn't believe how shy her husband was, who wouldn't even dare to lift her veil. It was Manasi who had to make the first move. Manasi's fingers found their way across the bed and touched Raj's hand, sending jolts of electric sensations down his spine. Even before the foreplay could commence, his climax was reached, witnessed only by his brand new Young India underwear. Manasi then asked him to lift the veil off her face. Gently, he moved over to lift the bright veil of her wedding dress covering her head and saw his beautiful wife for the first time. He has never imagined such beauty to even exist. Manasi looked straight into Raj's eyes which melted his heart. Raj gathered his wits and finally dared to draw closer to her. She expected him to kiss her lips; instead he went for her forehead. Manasi leaned in and gently rested her head on his shoulders so that he can feel the softness of her bosom on his chest. She then wrapped him in her arms and embraced him tight against herself. Raj had surrendered himself to his senses and went with the flow that Manasi had set for the two of them. She had only started to get excited as she managed to pull herself onto his lap. She starts moaning sensually and it was something that Raj had never experienced before. He was amazed as if witnessing the eighth wonder of the world. Her sharp scarlet nails dug into his back as she got more aroused. Manasi flipped open the buttons of her blouse with nervous fingers as Raj grappled about her chest with his hungry lips. He tried to reach her left nipple but the cup of her bra intervened his path. His finger wrestled with the hooks of her bra behind her back, but was unsuccessful. Manasi then took charge and helped him with her own hands. Raj wanted to take a moment to have a complete look of her but she was already at the edge of an oral orgasm. Her moaning sounds reverberated through the entire room. She climaxed with a loud sigh and Raj found himself witnessing a very unfamiliar situation.

She rested her head on his shoulder and asked him, "Is this your first time?"

Raj was speechless at the expert nature of her love making and responded hesitantly, "Yes and yours?"

"Do I look like a whore? Obviously, it was the first time for me too."

Raj couldn't believe her spontaneity but was happy to know that she had been a virgin too. But since the doubt had erupted in his mind, he needed the satisfaction of his own conformation. Raj looked deep into her eyes and headed straight for her right nipple. She couldn't resist him. She unbuttoned his sherwani and peeled it off of his bare skin, while he helped her get out of her heavy lehanga. Raj attacked the left nipple next, arousing her like a live volcano. Raj kissed her down her torso and reached the nape of her thighs. His lips teased and tingled her between the legs and she blew up in sensual reactions. He was careful not to rupture her hymen with his lips yet. He had never felt better. The final moment had come. She did not resisted, instead helped him attain the blessing of eternal joy. With a gentle thrust, Raj entered Manasi. Inadvertently, he said, "I Love you".

Manasi looked at him wordlessly and aided him in making more thrusts. Raj however, was too excited and aroused to contain himself and he came much before Manasi could get to her second orgasm. She was frustrated and kept trying the whole night to get his erection last longer but the pipe overflowed time after time, much before the usual climax.

Days passed but Raj's stamina could still not make the mark. He started taking all kinds of ayurvedic medicines but received no concrete results.

Slowly, the sweet bliss of their new marriage started crumbling.

CHAPTER 3
THE PRIMARY EVENT

One day Manasi went for shopping, but she was in a very angry mood. Anger had become her constant companion since she had gotten married to Raj. Raj followed her quietly to the market, much to her displeasure.

Manasi barked at him, “Don’t chase me.”

Raj had trailed a little behind her, as she marched on speedily.

Raj tried to convince her again, as he had been trying to do for days, “First listen to me; you are walking very fast and shouting at me unnecessarily too.”

She was disgusted, “Your walk is as slow as your thinking.”

Raj took some long strides to cover the distance between himself and Manasi.

Trying to placate her, he said, “I always try to make you happy but there is no end to your fault-finding in me”.

“Why don’t you understand, I don’t want to live a life of compromise?”

“I am trying my best. But how do you expect me to change in just a day?”

They had reached the shopping plaza and climbed the stairs leading up to the front entrance.

“You’re all talk and no action. You never try.”

“If I hadn’t tried, then how would I be here at 11 A.M. in the morning to see all the shops unopened yet?”

“You think that everyone is as lazy as you, don’t you? Come”.

They passed by some closed shops.

"See? None of the shops have opened yet."

Manasi, who still walked a step ahead of Raj, found a shop which was open.

"See! That shop is open."

Raj stared in the face of failure, yet again. He followed her dejectedly into the shop. The shopkeeper was engaged in a conversation with his wife over the phone. The size of his paunch hanging over the belt was big enough to hold a pair of twins. He had two sales girls standing obediently beside him.

He was busy addressing his wife's enquiry, who doubted that he was having an affair with the sales girls in the shop.

He tried to explain, "There is no salesgirl in the shop. Last time when you came here to check, what did you find? Nothing. There is still no girl in the shop. I will come at lunch time. I will come. Yes, soon."

On finding two new customers in the shop, he concluded the talk on the phone saying, "We will talk later," and disconnected the phone.

Raj wondered how someone could manage multiple women at the same time when just one weighed heavy on himself.

The shopkeeper turned to them and greeted, "Good morning, madam. How can I help you?"

Raj was taken aback as the shopkeeper had only greeted her. Experienced shopkeepers knew exactly whom to target and from whom the money would come.

Manasi responded saying, "Show me some salwar suits."

The shopkeeper guided them to the customer's bench and started showing suit pieces to her.

"See this one madam, this suit is very good. It is soft and beautiful and costs only Rs.1,225. It is the latest trend. It will make you look like the Bollywood actress Katrina Kaif."

Manasi was not convinced, "No. Show me some other piece."

She eyed another piece on the shelf and demanded, "Take that one out."

The shopkeeper appreciatively conceded, "Excellent choice, madam. This one is good too. You will look beautiful in this, at the mere cost of Rs.995."

To grab Raj's attention he added, "Doesn't it look good, sir?"

Raj recalled that Manasi had a similar set back home and said, "You already have something like this."

Manasi didn't like his interference and said, "Please don't disturb me."

A dormant volcano still houses a lot of threatening hot lava.

A regular looking young guy, about twenty years in age, entered the shop then. He had a frail body and looked like a local goon. The moment he saw Manasi, he couldn't stop staring at her. Perhaps her beauty had captured him. Manasi was busy browsing through her purchase options. Raj was also trying to figure when his woman will be satisfied and get what she desired.

The shopkeeper responded each of her whims and encouraged her all through with his 'Yes Madam's.'

"Show me another one."

Her demands kept increasing as her eyes surveyed the shop for potential purchases, "Show me that one."

The Shopkeeper teased Raj saying, "First, both of you confirm whether she already has this set at home or not."

Carving the shopkeeper's attention towards herself, Manasi said, "You show me what I ask for."

The remark stung Raj deeply who felt himself reduced to

the function of a Wallet, present there only to sponsor her shopping. His questions and opinions had no place or value.

Meanwhile the other guy tried to grab the shopkeeper's attention. Interrupting the scene, he said, "Show me that one".

The shopkeeper, in the greed to mature one sale quickly, turned to Raj and said, "Sir, Sir, does she own this one already? Is it okay?"

Manasi cleared her throat to bring his attention back to her. "Yes, show it to me…this one".

The shopkeeper was intelligent, for he wanted to make a sale to the couple, while also retain the other customer.

He responded to the other guy saying, "Brother, please give me two minutes. I will be with you in no time."

The guy nodded, expressing his approval.

The shopkeeper returned his attention to Manasi, "Okay Madam, tell me."

"Yes, show me this suit on yourself."

The shopkeeper put the salwar suit against himself and replied happily, "You will look like the actress Bipasha Basu in this. It is the choicest pick."

Manasi didn't like the border of this suit and asked for another option. The shopkeeper quickly came out with another piece.

"Madam, this one is for Rs.1,625. Really good, madam. It was worn by the Miss World Aishwarya Rai herself. It is real good. Best price, Rs.1,625 only."

Manasi, not convinced still, asked for another option, "Show me something in the latest design. I want a fashionable piece."

Pointing at a suit hanging at the shelf she demanded, "Show me that one."

The shopkeeper turned to look at her new choice.

"Madam, this one? Wait, I'll take it out for you right away."

As soon as the shopkeeper lunged towards the shelf, the young guy got the opportunity to snatch the beautiful mangalsutra off Manasi's neck and made a run for it. Raj, Manasi, the shopkeeper and the sales girls had all been drawn in by the desired suit piece when he took his chance to commit the crime. He had no care for Manasi's beauty, but only for the expensive piece of jewellery on her neck, which he could trade for money and feed himself thereafter. Manasi was struck with horror. Her hand reached up to her throat.

"Oh! What has he done!?"

Raj was clueless about the whole ordeal and asked, "What happened, Manasi?"

Manasi was quick to realize that her mangalsutra was stolen by the boy who had been standing beside her. "That boy stole my mangalsutra!" she exclaimed.

Raj couldn't believe that a theft has taken place, right under his nose. He was still trying to figure out what needs to be done when Manasi barked at him, "What are you looking at? Go and catch the thief."

The shopkeeper joined in and yelled, "Go brother! Thief Thief Thief Thief! Catch that thief!"

"Was that a thief?"

Raj ran out of the shop and shouted, "Catch that thief."

Not one bystander cared for the victim or catching the thief. A crowd quickly gathered around to watch the chase but none did anything to help. In India, people fear getting involved in any task which could result in a Police case. It had come down to just Raj and the thief. Raj chased him around whatever twists and turns he took for about a kilometer, before his stomach started to ache. Raj couldn't bear the pain and finally stopped in his chase. The thief heaved a sigh of relief when he found out that his pursuit had ended and he had been successful in his theft.

Raj made his way back to the shop to pick Manasi up, but found out upon reaching that she had already left.

CHAPTER 4

A NIGHT TO REMEMBER

Raj bothered about her and raced his brains as to where she could have gone, the whole way back home. On reaching his house, he found her on the terrace, hanging wet clothes on wires to dry.

After a moment of relief, he questioned, "Manasi, why did you leave me there and come home by yourself?"

"What else should I have done? Stood there and let people laugh at me till you came back? One meagre little thin-bodied thief stole my necklace and what did you do? Stood there dumbfounded and let him run away with my jewellery. You are nothing but a loser."

"I chased him Manasi, but my stomach started hurting. What could I have done after that?"

"Stomach ache is just an excuse; you can't hide yourself behind it. You are a loser."

"Your taunts will not bring that necklace back."

"I feel trapped in this marriage. Why didn't I lose you with that necklace too?"

"Don't be so stressed out. With the next month's salary, I will buy you another necklace."

"I'd rather have another husband, than another necklace."

Manasi stormed off and hurriedly climbed down the stairs. Raj followed her but she was in no mood to talk to him.

"Manasi…Manasi, listen…Manasi, please listen to me."

She walked swiftly across the huge balcony, Raj in pursuit.

"Manasi don't make a big issue out of this."

"I don't want to talk to you."

Manasi entered the house and closed the door behind her.

Raj pleaded from outside, "Manasi open the door please. Manasi!"

She yelled from inside, "Get lost."

The dormant volcano had now bubbled over and the sky was overcast with dense volcanic clouds of fire and ash.

"Manasi."

Raj made repeated efforts to convince her to open the door, but she didn't even respond. Raj waited for a long time, but the burning lava had now over flown the rim and this volcano was not going to cool down anytime soon. Raj spent the whole night on the terrace, thinking what could be done to solve the issue. The whole night passed by in vain and Raj remained sleepless till the sun rose again.

Chapter 5
ALL DOORS CLOSED

In the morning, he made his way out to eat something, as he hadn't even had dinner the night before and his stomach murmured with starvation. After having some jalebis and curd, he came back home. As he climbed up to the first floor, where he lived with Manasi, he overheard her talking on the phone with her mother back in Kanpur.

"Why should I care what your neighbour has done with you? You listen to me. I had asked you to get me married to that U.S. based engineer. But no, you wanted me to marry this stupid loser. You have destroyed my whole life."

Her mother tried her best to calm her down, "Look Manasi."

"Look what? He could not even save his wife's mangalsutra. You think he'll be able to look after me, my entire life? Listen to how he has been with me all this while."

She narrated the entire story her grievances to her mother. These were the events where Raj got a special medal from her, not for being a good husband but for being an absolute failure.

(MEDAL 1: LAZY NUMBER ONE)

"This has been the most usual feature. Daily in the morning, I start waking him up at 6 A.M. and he never gets up before 7 A.M. He walks instead of jogging. He has no enthusiasm for life. He is a lazy man."

(MEDAL 2: LOW STANDARD)

"I didn't have a clue where he was taking me, the day before yesterday. Since his mood was great, I didn't want to bother him by asking. To my surprise, I landed at a Bhindi Bazaar. As soon as I entered the place, I stepped into a filthy, water-logged mud patch.

I said, "Chi! How dirty this place is. Where you have brought me?"

He argued saying, "To purchase potatoes."

I asked, "Is this a place to purchase potatoes? We could have gone to the supermarket. Look how filthy and mud-covered these potatoes are. How can you ever hope to eat these potatoes?"

Instead of seeing reason, he tried to convince me, "But look how much fresh these potatoes are!"

"Mom, I had to leave the market without saying a word."

(MEDAL 3: MR. LATE)

"Once we had decided to go for my favorite actor Salman Khan's movie, Tubelight. He had to leave office early that evening, pick me up from home and reach the cinema hall on time for the 6 P.M. show.

I waited eagerly all day and when he finally arrived in the evening, I told him, "If we miss this film, I will see you."

'We reached Novelty Cinemas, which was so overcrowded with Salman Khan's fans already, that it seemed impossible to get the tickets. Raj parked the scooter on the road and made his way to the ticket window. As soon as he reached the window, they put up the sign 'Housefull'.

Raj walked back to me bent and dejected and told me that

the show was house full.

I told him angrily, “It is all because of you that we missed the film.”

“Mom, my husband is the real tube-light, always late. Late *Lateef.*”

(MEDAL 4: UNCIVILIZED)

“Mom, he always eats with his fingers, in my absence. I don’t know why people eat with their fingers. It’s so unhygienic. Raj is such an uncivilized man.”

(MEDAL 5: UNROMANTIC)

“One day I was in a great mood as Raj told me he’ll take me to Hazratganj for ganj-ing (roaming). I then suggested, “Come on Raj. Let’s go to a good restaurant.”

Raj replied, “There is one restaurant here which is my favourite. Let’s go there.” He hailed for a rickshaw and directed him to take us there.

On approaching a sub-standard roadside restaurant, Raj said, “Rickshaw, stop here. We have arrived, Manasi.”

He stepped down from the rickshaw and told me, “Look, this is my favourite restaurant.”

I couldn’t control my temper and yelled at him, “Raj, I thought that you would take me to some five star hotel. Do you really think that I’d like to eat here? What sort of a man are you? Rickshaw, please take me onward, pedal away!”

Raj cried out from behind, “Arrey Manasi…listen to me…Manasi. Manasi…please, Manasi. Manasi…listen to me…Manasi.”

Raj kept calling after me but I didn’t stop there, even for a minute.”

(MEDAL 6: STUPID LOSER)

"Mom, I cannot live with Raj for even a single moment more. He's such a stupid Loser. I hate him. God knows what sins I had committed in my previous birth to have secured such a husband."

Manasi was so engrossed in the phone call that she didn't realise that Raj had come to stand right behind her, listening to all that she said.

Once she became aware of it she spoke into the phone quietly, "Mom, I will talk to you later."

Before Manasi could give him an excuse, Raj opened the door and entered his home.

Manasi disconnected the phone and entered behind him. They didn't speak to each other the entire day and slept on the opposite ends of the bed that night. Raj slept while Manasi lay awake thinking of what could be done next.

Chapter 6
D DAY

The sun rose at the same time to another regular day. Manasi went for her usual morning jog, but without Raj this time as he was sleeping and she thought better not to disturb him.

Raj sat anxiously at the dining table for breakfast to be served as he was getting late for office.

He asked Manasi, "Give me something to eat."

She brought two omelettes and 4 slices of bread to the table.

Raj didn't like bread and omelette.

"You know I prefer parathas and sabzi for breakfast, then why have you brought me this English breakfast which gives no nutrition."

"Parathas have only carbohydrates and our body needs more proteins than carbs. I insist that you eat this protein diet."

Raj threw her a look, silently expressing that she couldn't force him to eat something which he didn't like. She was busy in the kitchen pouring milk into a glass for him when he got up and left for office without having eaten anything. When she brought the glass of hot milk to the table, she was surprised not to find him. She couldn't believe that Raj had left just like that.

Raj reached his office late as usual. As soon as he had put his things at his desk, he was called in by the Regional Manager (RM). His gut feeling said that something really terrible was going to happen. The RM closed a file at his desk as soon as he saw Raj enter his office. The expression on his face suddenly turned for the worse as his eyes met with Raj's.

"Ever since you've gotten married you don't seem to concentrate on your work. You are not sincere anymore. Last month, the company slipped out on a big deal just because of you. We have suffered more losses than merited gains from you. The company cannot take this anymore. You are fired. Get out."

Raj was shocked and exited the office dejectedly. Losing the job was one problem but the bigger dilemma was telling Manasi about it. His good salary was the only thing that had kept her from leaving him and now that was lost too. Raj's mind cooked up all sorts of ideas all day of how to confront her, what to say her, what could be the best moment to reveal this to her, where should he say it and what could be the odds that she remains calm, even after listening to all of it.

Meanwhile at home, Manasi received a letter, handed to her by the courier man. She opened the letter and immediately got annoyed. She called up Raj right away.

Raj picked up the phone with a sombre, "Hello."

"Raj?"

"Yes, Manasi."

"What is this, Raj?"

"Will you tell me what happened?"

"I just received a notice that your bank installment has not been deposited."

"Yes, because we have been spending a lot in setting up and decoration of the house and just last month you purchased a new sofa. All the money was spent over that."

"Raj, you should have told me that there is no money in your bank account."

"I am really sorry on that account; however I have another

bad news, besides this."

"What else can I expect from you? Say it." Sarcasm dripped from her tone.

Raj hesitated a little before saying, "I have been fired from job."

Manasi was quiet for a second, as if she had got the shock of her life-time before saying, "Fired from job? Huuuuuffff." The phone line then went dead from her end.

Raj didn't call her back at that instant as he knew very well that it was not the best time to confront her. Instead, he passed the whole day roaming the city and sitting at various places, killing time and getting his guts up to return home and face his wife.

The sky had started to grow dark and the street lights shone golden above the roads. Raj opened the door of his house with a spare key that he had gotten made for himself, the original being with Manasi. The place was enveloped in darkness. He switches on the lights Manasi was not there. He called out her name, but got no response. He checked all the rooms, the kitchen, the corridor, the washroom, the terrace, etc. but she was nowhere to be found. Giving some consolation to his heart, he tried to convince himself that she could have gone shopping and would be back any second. He took his shoes off and eased himself down on the couch. His eyes searched for the T.V.'s remote control and found it lying on the table. He reached out for it and angled it towards the T.V. set. Just then his eyes caught a yellow slip pasted to the T.V. screen. Inadvertently, he pealed it off and started reading,

I am going far away from you. Please don't try to find me. I cannot spend my whole life with a loser.

Raj immediately dug out the phone from his pocket and called Manasi. Her phone was switched off. He then called

Manasi's mother.

She picked up with a droning, "Hello!"

"Are Mummy…Mummy, Manasi is not at home…do you have any idea where she could have gone?"

Manasi's mother hesitated, "She took my word that I will not tell you where she is."

"I am her husband. I have all the right to know where my wife is."

"But I gave her my promise."

"Is your promise bigger than your daughter's life?"

She kept quiet for a while before saying, "She has gone to Mumbai."

"Mumbai!"

Chapter 7
CITY OF POSSIBILITIES

It would sound clichéd to call Mumbai the New York City of India, but that is what describes our city of dreams the best. It is the city that never sleeps, that is always up and about, a city with a spirit of gold accompanied by the determination of a never say die attitude, even in the wake of terrorist attacks and natural calamities. Could the city bring the married life of Raj and Manasi back on its wheels?

Raj called his childhood friend Monty and narrated the whole story to him. Monty asked him to come to Mumbai right away. He showed Raj around the city in an attempt to distract him by telling him what to do and what not to do in this city. While having dinner one night, Monty looked at his dispirited friend remorsefully. Monty had served almost all the chapattis to himself, leaving only a few for Raj.

Monty advised him, "To tame a woman, you need money and for money, you need a job. You do one thing." Monty reached for his wallet in his pocket and looked through it for a business card. On finding it, he handed it to Raj and said, "Take this card and go for an interview tomorrow."

Raj took the card and looked at it hopefully. This card could land him a job and a job would bring with it some stability in his life.

The next morning, he reached the exact address but was terribly late. In Lucknow city, travelling a distance of 15 kilometers only took about 30 minutes at max, but he hadn't imagined how long it could take him to cover the same distance in the city of Mumbai. He first had to take an auto to the local Railway Station, get in a queue to buy a ticket, then figure out which train would go where. He then had to alight at the chosen railway station and search for rickshaw again which could take him to the office location. Mumbai city is such that it checks the patience of anybody who is new to it. He followed the routine and reached the office late by two hours. As he just was entering the office building when a watchman stopped him.

The guard inquired, "Where are you going, sir?"

Raj, covered in sweat and anxiety, replied, "I have an interview at the Bee Positive Retail Company."

The watchman intercom-ed the office to enquire about the interviews and passed the information onto Raj saying, "Sir you are late, the interviews have already finished and a suitable candidate has been chosen too."

Raj's disappointments were never ending; even the City of Possibilities had failed him poorly. Raj took a taxi to Marine Drive and sat there watching the skyline of Mumbai. A single thought invaded his mind,

"Manasi, where are you in this big city?"

CHAPTER 8
MOTH IN A COCOON

Weekends are the time when people with corporate lifestyles take some time off and are found on the beach running, skipping, walking and spending time with their families. Monty was no different from this fraternity. For him, life was fun and he lived life is if there was no tomorrow. On a Sunday, Monty woke Raj up and dragged him to the beach to jog. After they had covered a distance of about 500 meters, Raj's stomach started to hurt again. Monty kept up his pace and didn't realize for a few moments that Raj was no longer accompanying him. He turned around and found Raj a few paces back, bent double, holding his stomach.

"Raj, what happened? Got tired so quickly?" he asked, running back to his side.

Raj pressed the side of his stomach with his hand and said, "It's the usual stomach-ache again."

Monty questioned with a hint of concern, "Stomach-ache?"

Raj tried to explain between long gasps of breath, "Whenever I run for a little longer than I am used to, my stomach starts hurting."

"For how long have you been having this problem," Monty enquired.

Raj took a deep breath before answering, "For as long as I can remember."

"Have you consulted a doctor yet?" Monty asked curiously.

Raj flatly said, "No."

"What sort of a man are you? Until you show yourself to a doctor, how will you know what the problem is?" Monty asked in a stern but even tempered tone.

Raj had never seen it as a serious problem and had grown accustomed to it as a usual phenomenon. Thus, he replied, "It gets well on its own soon."

Monty was exasperated and tried to convince him, "Raj, this is not the way. A problem is solved only when it is tackled head-on. If you don't solve the problem in time, it will only increase. Come, I will fix an appointment with Dr. Bamboli for you."

He lent his arm towards Raj for support.

CHAPTER 9
THE MOTH FINDS A WAY OUT OF THE COCOON

Dr. Bamboli, a very senior psychologist, took a deep look at Raj's reports and then looked up to see him in the eye.

"From your reports, one thing is very clear Raj; you don't have any medical problem at all."

Both Raj and Monty were taken aback, Raj, particularly, took it hard.

"This is a psychological problem. Imagine your body like a computer. What happens when a virus enters the computer? It crashes. In the same way, a virus has entered your own mind. Medical research has proven that our body behaves vis-à-vis the instructions released from the mind. In your sub-conscious mind, this fact has been registered that whenever you run, your stomach will experience pain. So when you run in real life, your mind gives an instruction to your brain that your stomach is hurting, and thus you feel pain."

Monty nodded half in understanding, half in agreement and asks, "Sir, the logic makes sense but is there a solution to it?"

"I am sorry but this is a disease that cannot be cured by any doctor in this world. It's in your own hands and you'll need to cure it yourself," he said.

Raj was astonished, "I do?"

"Yes, it is simple logic. You'll need to eliminate the thought of pain from your mind forever. It's like loading new software in the computer, which tells you that there is no problem in your body anymore. Everything is fine. Yes, we can motivate you externally up to a certain level, but ultimately it's up to you how you manage to delete that thought. In fact, I would suggest that you start jogging regularly and increase the distance by a little margin every day. You are absolutely fit and fine otherwise. Thank you."

The doctor's apparent logical and scientific reasoning seemed to convince Raj and changed the way he thought about himself.

CHAPTER 10
ANGELS AND DEMONS

Monty fixed an interview for Raj at his own office. As they were crossing the Bombay Library, Monty tried to upload a new software in his mind - "How to be confident?"

"Don't panic for the interview. You understand what I am saying? I am with you. I have arranged for everything at the office. You just be confident," he said, in an attempt to motivate him.

On reaching his workplace, Monty directed Raj towards the CEO's chamber, while placing himself just outside of the glass partition and tried to peek in. From the corner of his eyes, he saw Mr. Kamat entering the office. He quickly moved to his seat, before Mr. Kamat could get a chance to notice him. The whole office went silent at Mr. Kamat's entry, as if some ghost had descended into the building and people bowed down to pray for God's help.

After sometime, Raj walked out with a sorrowful face. Monty had his eyes fixed on the CEO's door and when he saw Raj, it appeared to him that another defeat had been added to his list of failures. Raj walked up to Monty's desk.

Monty could guess what must have happened at the CEO's chamber and said, "Your face says that you failed again. What happened?"

"I messed it up."

"I knew it…I knew that you will commit some blunder again," he said disappointedly.

Raj laughed out just then. The software that Monty had

been trying to upload, had certainly found its place in Raj's mind.

"You are joking, aren't you? You're joking, you bugger. Haha, my love. Good, I am so happy for you," Monty exclaimed with happiness.

"Who is Kamat Sir? The boss asked me to report to him," Raj enquired after thanking him.

"Look around; there is only one devil in this office. I am sure you will identify him." Monty rolled his eyes.

In every office, there is always that one person, who nobody likes, who neither works himself nor allows anyone to work either. Raj turned his head around and surveyed the room before his eyes rested on a grouchy middle aged man. He had recognised the Demon. Raj could see him shoving papers here and there. It seemed he was busy drafting some official letters. Everyone in the office knew that even one letter in the day was too much work for him. Raj couldn't wait any longer as he had to meet him and start his workday.

He walked upto him and greeted politely, "Good morning, sir."

Mr. Kamat was busy writing, or made it seem like he was involved in something very important. Raj made an effort again, "Sir, I am Raj."

Raj had tested Mr. Kamat's patience and had now to pay back for his karma.

Kamat yelled at him in anger, "So what? I don't care whether you are Raj or Rajesh Khanna. Please don't disturb me, I am working. Okay?"

Raj was stunned, but decided to approach him another way. He said, "Sir, I have been asked to meet you."

"People don't even give me the freedom to work in peace. Tell me, how I can help you?" Kamat said frustratedly.

Raj explained the situation calmly to him, "Sir, I have

joined the office just today."

"You could have told me that earlier."

"Sir, you didn't gave me chance."

"You know Computers?"

"Sir, I am an MCA from JNU."

"What does an MCA have to do with Computers?"

"Sir, MCA stands for Masters in Computer Application."

The whole office smiled silently as Kamat grew furious.

"If you are so smart then why have you come here? You should have gone to America. Nothing will happen for you in this country. I have grown tired doing the same work for eighteen years. The more you work, the more work you will get further. No rewards and no recognition."

Raj was not interested in his displeasure with working and wanted to get out of that zone as soon as possible.

"Sir, please explain my tasks to me."

"I will come and explain everything; you can go sit at your work station for now."

"Thank you, sir."

Raj walked back to Monty and the other colleagues who had been waiting to welcome him properly. They had only started making introductions when Mr. Rokade (the angel of the office) entered. Rokade was in his forties and seemed like a jolly natured man. He looked like one of those men for whom life was more important than work and that's the reason why all the staff members at the office loved him.

Rokade, beaming at everyone, asked, "What's going on? Everyone is in jolly mood today."

Monty stepped forward and said, "Sir, Raj has joined our office today."

Rokade smiled at Raj and greeted him saying, "That's great. Welcome, Raj!"

Raj felt the infectious nature of his happy spirit and said,

"Thank you so much sir."

Monty then introduced Raj to Mr. Rokade, "Raj, this is Rokade sir."

Rokade gestured towards Raj and said, "Whenever you need me, you come talk to me without any hesitation."

Raj nodded, while others smiled.

Rokade bid farewell to the group and continued walking towards his own cabin, "See you guys, enjoy."

Raj made many other acquaintances that day, the three musketeers of the office Srivastava, Mishraji and Guptaji; Kamini, the hottest girl at office who was also Monty's love interest; and Lallan Singh, the Chugalbaaz of the office. Everyone greeted Raj and welcomed him with warm hearts.

CHAPTER 11

MOTH MUST MAKE AN EFFORT

The morning alarm woke Monty up, as Raj kept sleeping. He gave Raj a kick to jolt him awake, but in vain. He sat up in his bed and started shaking him vigorously with his hands. Raj responded with a quick reply without opening his eyes, "Let me sleep for five more minutes."

Monty couldn't take it anymore and went straight to the bathroom. He filled a whole bucket with water and carried it back to Raj's bedside.

"If you don't get up, I am going to release the river Ganges onto you."

There was still no reply from Raj. Monty lifted the bucket up and emptied it over him. Raj woke with a start and sat up on the bed.

"What have you done?" he asked startled.

"Brother, it's 6 A.M. already and you should be on the beach."

Raj got off the bed and walked begrudgingly to the bathroom.

After a while, he walked out all dry and dressed in a new track suit. To his surprise, he found Monty sleeping.

"Hey, will you not accompany me?" he asked.

Monty said sleepily, "I run only on Sundays and it is your software that is damaged, not mine by the way. Running is your requirement, not mine. Let me stay and finish your Sunny Leone dreams. You go."

Raj took a full round of 5 kilometres at the beach. When

he got exhausted, he chose to sit on a rock near the shore. Beside him on another rock, there sat a handicapped boy who silently looked at all the runners and joggers around him with empty eyes. One of his legs was crippled and his walking stick lay nearby. He seemed to have just entered his teen years. Raj tried to make conversation with him but he seemed disinterested. Raj went quiet after a while and joined him in watching others run on the beach. An old man came jogging in their direction and was greeted by his old wife with open arms. Both of them walked away together. Raj couldn't help but reminisce about Manasi hugging him. He remembered how Manasi had always wanted him to be fit. He envisioned and set it down in his brain that he would get Manasi back if only he could make himself more sporty and fit. He smiled at the thought and got up from the rock. The handicapped boy's followed him off of the rock and onto the jogging path, till he disappeared into the distance.

After completing a brisk run, Raj headed back home. On the way, he came across some people exiting a gymnasium. Raj looked up at the gym's poster which had all the details regarding the membership, timings, personal trainers, etc. The gym's curriculum interested him and he walked closer to read the fine print when suddenly, he overheard a familiar voice.

"Auto!"

Raj recognized the voice immediately and turned to look in that direction. He caught a glimpse of his wife Manasi, taking her seat in the auto. All blood drained from his body. It took him a second or two to come to this senses, after which he called out her name loudly and moved in her direction. The final moment had come. He shouted, "Manasi," but the auto had already started moving without her having heard him. He called after her again, "Manasi...Manasi...Manasi," but the auto didn't stop, neither did it slow down. Perhaps the engine of the auto rickshaw was too loud for Manasi to have heard his voice.

Raj ran back home and found Monty shaving, getting ready for work.

Raj entered the house all excited. "Monty…Monty."

Monty called out from his washroom, "Yes?"

"You are here. Monty, I am very happy."

"Why?" he asked.

"I found Manasi!" Raj exclaimed blushing.

Monty set the blade down and asked surprised, "What are you saying? Where did you find her?"

"At the Gym right around the corner, I saw her leaving the place just now."

"What was she doing there?" Monty asked curiously.

"I believe that she has joined that gym." Raj assumed.

Monty suggested, "Then you should join that gym too."

Raj couldn't contain his happiness. During the office hours that very day, Raj called up the gym manager, paid his membership fee online and got ready to meet his wife during the evening session at the gym.

CHAPTER 12

WHEN YOU ASK IT SHALL BE GIVEN

Raj couldn't contain his excitement all day and felt like he was on seventh heaven. He walked through the gym's gates in the evening and headed straight for the reception. A beautiful girl greeted him saying, "Welcome to Five-fitness gymnasium. How can I help you sir?"

"I had applied online for a membership," Raj confessed.

"Give me a moment sir, let me check the data," she said as she punched Raj's name into the computer and searched for his account. On finding his details, she continued, "Yes, I see that you are our newest member here. You can start your workout right away."

"Can you help me with something?" Raj asked.

"Yes sir, why not?"

"Can you tell me what time does Manasi come here?"

"Sir, there are more than 2000 members in our gym and there must be at least a dozen Manasi's here," the receptionist explained. "It'll be very difficult to find the one that you're looking for. Besides, our gym's privacy policy does not allow us to disclose a member's personal details to another member."

Raj gave it a thought and nodded, "I understand."

"Be regular to the gym and I am sure it won't take you much time to find her," the receptionist said, winking at him.

"Thank you for the suggestion," Raj said.

"The pleasure is ours," she replied with a smile.

Raj turned to go, but ran into a girl just then who had

been walking towards the reception. She had her earphones popped in and was too lost in some song to avoid the collision. She lost her balance and would have tumbled backwards if not for Raj who was quick to react and held her by her waist. For a moment they couldn't take their eyes off each other. He noticed that she was wearing an orange bundy with Reebok slacks, while she seemed lost in the simplicity and purity of Raj's expression. Her smoky eyelashes retained Raj's attention for a while. Neither of them said sorry as they straightened and separated form each other. The girl's eyes seemed so deep that Raj couldn't stop looking at them. The black mascara around her eyes had made them look even more beautiful. Raj noticed that she was the same height as himself and carried herself with a lot of confidence.

Just then Sam, a body builder, entered the gym. He noticed the two of them looking at each other, which distracted this girl's attention and she turned to looked at him. At this moment, Raj's attention moved to the perfectly proportionate figure of her body. Aaliya, the girl, turned to give Raj one last look before heading towards the gym area. Sam followed her and Raj followed the two of them.

It was very loud inside the gym. Everyone was busy lifting weights and doing all sorts of exercises. This was a completely new world for Raj. Since it was his first day, he found himself confused and indecisive about where to start. He spotted an old man walking on the treadmill and decided to follow suit. It appeared to be the easy option. Before he reached the treadmill, he turned to look at the collision-girl again. She was engaged in stretching exercises at a little distance. The girl could feel his gaze on herself too. Raj was so tantalised by the attraction that he felt towards this girl that he forgot about Manasi for a moment. His mind started playing games with him.

Raj pondered over the thought, Who is better?; Manasi or this girl whom I have just met for the first time. His mind argued that Manasi was his wife; he should not be looking at other women. What are you doing? Manasi comes to this gym too. If someone were to reveal to her that you were looking at this girl, will Manasi like it? Never. Don't look at her. Don't look at her.

His mind was still fighting and grappling with these thoughts when he took a wrong step over the treadmill. He stumbled and fell with a loud bang and was dragged off to the floor. He became the object of attention and ridicule for everyone else at the gym. Raj heard Sam laughing loudly. His laughter seemed to say, "God punished you for looking at the girl whom I like." As people continued to laugh and nobody came to his rescue, he stood up and walked out of the gym area. The girl, who had witnessed his embarrassment closely, followed him out.

Raj was sipping cool water, standing beside the water filter when she joined him.

"Are you a new member?" she asked.

Raj nodded in affirmative.

"I believe you need help."

"I don't think I'll be able to do any of this."

"Why not?" she asked curiously.

"Don't you see what happened?"

"Yes I did and I also noticed where your gaze was."

Raj's secret intentions were revealed and he felt slightly ashamed.

"Come, I will help you out." She grabbed hold of his hand and dragged him back inside.

She then started explaining a workout routine to him. "We will start with some warm-up exercises. Just follow closely the exercises that I am doing, okay? Bend your body to the right side first. On my count…1, 2, 3, 4, 5, 6. Now do the same with the left side. 1, 2, 3, 4, 5, 6, 7, 8, 9, 10."

She made him do some stretching exercises then, like the Seated trapezius stretch, Shoulder stretch, Triceps stretch, Lower back, Hip flexor stretch, Hamstring stretch, Quadriceps stretch and Calf stretch.

"Now we will move on to weights," she said, flushed from the warm-up and stretching.

She picked a twenty ounces weight and handed it to him, "Hold this."

Raj was not prepared for it.

"I have never lifted this much weight."

"When I can lift it, why can't you?" she said, trying to motivate him.

"It is very heavy." Raj was still hesitant.

"It's not very heavy. Lift it. Lift it. Once more, once more. Yes."

She drew close to help him lift. Her soft skin touched his stiff muscles. A tingling sensation rushed like a wave through his body. He felt as if coming closer to her was pushing him further away from Manasi, which he never wanted. Manasi was his wife, while this girl was nobody to him.

"What are you doing?"

"Helping you."

"By coming so close to me?" he asked nervously.

"This weight is a little too heavy for you. To help you lift it, I need to come closer to you."

Raj remembered the oath that he had taken at his marriage altar of never looking at another woman besides Manasi, after the wedding.

"I can't do it."

"No worries. Let's do bench exercises."

Raj wants to escape before the sacred arrangement between Manasi and himself could break.

"I will do nothing more today. I have to leave. Thank you

so much for your help. Goodbye."

Raj made his way out of the gym hurriedly. This girl, with her never-say-die attitude, followed him out.

The streets were lit with mild yellow incandescence emitting from the street lamps on either side. Raj felt as if he had made a narrow escape and heaved a sigh of relief for having kept the vows that he had made to Manasi at their wedding. Little did he know however, that while he was busy chasing his wife, another girl was chasing him.

A voice called out from behind, "Wait."

To his surprise, the girl had followed him down to the street.

"What are you doing here?" he asked flustered.

"Going home."

"Your house is on this road?"

"Yes, will you accompany me?"

Before Raj could say anything, she said "Thank you" and started walking. Soon, she started firing a string of questions at him.

"You didn't tell me your name."

He knew it was impossible to escape her, so he surrendered.

"My name is Raj."

"I am Aaliya."

He thought that her name should have been *Aailah* for the wonder that she was.

"Is this your first time at a gym?" She shot another question.

"Where do you stay?" And another.

"I asked, where do you stay?" she repeated, when he didn't answer.

The desperate girl needed her answers, while Raj was trying to evade all her questions. She had decided to make this poor guy, half-dead with humiliation at the gym already, her target. She walked two strides ahead of him and spread her arms wide to block his way. He had no chance of escape.

"I know you feel attracted towards me. You like me, right? See, I am a straight forward girl and I want a straight forward answer. Do you like me or not?"

Raj was benumbed by her proposal. However, ever since the collision at the gym's reception, he had started preparing an answer in his head, anticipating that a situation like this would arise.

"Look Aaliya, I am married," he said decidedly.

"So what? I don't mind…I like you."

Raj couldn't believe his ears. This girl was absolutely mad, he thought. He tried again.

"Look, I love my wife very much."

She was a better psychologist than Dr. Bamboli could ever be. I was convinced of this with the statement that followed.

"If you love your wife so much, why were you staring at me?" she asked, cocking her head to one side.

Raj has no answer for it and decided to simply avoid her and move ahead. As things were not working for Aaliya, she decided on a different strategy and said, "Okay, fine. I will come to your house."

He was shocked at her response. "For what?"

"I will meet your wife."

Raj felt like he had met Lady Sherlock Holmes. She had some impressive detective skills. She insisted in her usual tone, "Come, let's go to your place."

Raj didn't budge an inch and said, "She is not at home."

"How can you be so sure of that? Let's go home and check," she demanded.

Lowering his head shamefully, he confessed, "She has left me."

Aaliya was surprised, "How can anyone leave a guy like

you?"

Raj kept quiet. Aaliya continued, "There must be some solid reason behind that. Tell me why?"

Raj didn't say a word still.

"If you want, you can share it with me," she said, trying to egg him on.

For a moment, Raj felt shaky whether he should reveal the grievances of his newly married life to a complete stranger or not, but soon he was overwhelmed by emotions bursting at the seams of his heart and vented them out to her.

He told Aaliya everything about himself and Manasi and their rocky married life, including a personal account of his wedding night. He couldn't comprehend why or how he was able to share his past in such detail with a girl he had just met earlier that evening. Aaliya listened to his story very patiently and attentively. He had never met anyone like her ever before.

Chapter 13

SOMETHINGS YOU CAN'T RESIST

The next morning, Raj found himself jogging on the street. He couldn't help but remember the whole conversation with Aaliya the night before. He even remembered the exact place where he left her and had now reached the same spot. He looked up at a building, wondering which of those apartments could belong to Aaliya, when suddenly someone ran into him, colliding with a bang. Raj couldn't believe the co-incidence, for it was Aaliya yet again.

She mumbled, "Arrey…Raj."

"Oh…no. You again," Raj said amazed.

Aaliya crossed her hands in mock anger and said, "Oh, I am so sorry."

Raj asked her, "What are you doing here?"

Aaliya said bluntly, "Chasing you."

"What?" Raj exclaimed, shocked even further.

Aaliya laughed lightly and explained, "Can't you see? I am jogging, too."

Raj replied frustratedly, "You could only find this place for jogging, in this big city."

"Raj this is my area and I can jog wherever I want," Aaliya said in a defensive tone.

They were now running in the same direction. Raj ordered, "You stop."

Aaliya was not one to obey, "Why should I stop?"

Raj gave up the battle, "Then I will stop."

Raj stopped and she trailed back to join him again.

"Why did you come back? You were running in that direction." He pointing his finger ahead.

Aaliya was quiet determined. "I have a question," she said.

One more question. God save me, he thought disinterestedly.

"I don't want to answer," he replied.

She didn't care, there was no escape for him.

"Why were you looking at my house back there?"

"I was not looking at your house."

"You were. I saw your eyes searching for me."

"It's your faulty thinking."

"There is no faulty thinking."

Raj felt irritated and said, "You perceive everything wrongly, Aaliya. It's not what you think, there is nothing like that."

"I understand now. When girls show attitude, boys run after them but when girls go after boys, they get the chance to show their own attitude."

This girl is mad. Run. Raj confirmed the fact in his head and started running ahead of her.

"Wait." Aaliya chased after him again. Both of them stopped beside a Tennis Stadium wall. Raj lunged towards the wall, gasping heavily. Aaliya rested her back against it too. Tempering his breath, he repleated, "I am married. Don't follow me."

"Raj when a woman leaves a man, she never comes back."

"She will come back."

"Why do you have such confidence that she will?"

"She comes to our gym."

Sudden surprise shone clear on her face. As a result, a new question followed. "Our gym? What's her name?"

"Manasi."

"There are seven Manasi's in our gym. Which Manasi are

you talking about?"

"The one from Kanpur."

Aaliya frowned, straining to remember the Manasi I was referring to.

"Manasi from Kanpur. Is it the short girl?"

"You know her?"

"She is my trainee."

"Will you help me?"

"That I can't say."

Saying this, Aaliya moved off. She now wanted him to chase her. Raj kept looking in her direction, wondering what to do next.

Chapter 14
DESTINY IS INEVITABLE

Later that morning, Raj stood at a Bus Stop, waiting for his company bus. Suddenly, he saw Aaliya approaching and quickly turned his back to her. Aaliya, not knowling that Raj was there, hailed for an Auto-rikshaw and quickly stepped into it. Raj was looking at her from the corner of his eye and noticed that her purse fell from her bag, down on the road, unnoticed by Aaliya herself. Before he could act, the auto had already moved on. Though, Raj yelled after her yet she didn't hear. Raj picked up the purse in time and tried to look for Auto-rikshaws himself in order to follow her, but no one stopped for him as they were all occupied. Flustered, Raj looked around and saw her auto stopping at a traffic signal about 100 meters away. He made a run for it, but as soon as he covered half the distance, the signal turned green and the auto lurched forward. Aaliya was busy talking into her mobile phone with someone and couldn't hear Raj 's hollers. Raj continued to run after her. Raj was now about 20 meters behind her auto. Aaliya cut the call and popped the earphones in to listen to her favorite songs on her android phone. The roads were busy and congested during the peak hours of the morning and Raj found himself closing up to the auto numerous times. He called out to her yet again, but she couldn't hear him. Finally, the auto stopped.

Aaliya stepped out and asked for the fare. "Bhaiya, how much?"

The auto-driver replied, "200 only, madam."

Aaliya rummaged through her bag, but couldn't find her purse. "Where is my purse? Do you know where my purse is. Where did it go?" She started panicking.

Raj finally managed to reach up to the auto. Gasping heavily he said, "Aaliya, your purse."

"Raj!?" Aaliya exclaimed in surprise. She took the purse from him and gave the auto driver his due. "Where did you find my purse?"

"You dropped it at the Bus Stop."

"You came running all the way here."

"Yes, I did."

"No way, that's impossible! Do you know, you just covered about 10 kilometers, running."

He couldn't believe his ears. "10 kilometers?"

"Yes, Mahim is 10 kilometers from Juhu."

"But how could I have run that far, that too without any pain, whatsoever?"

"Focus. You were driven by the sole motive to give me my purse. There was no other thought in your mind to distract or demotivate you. Our mind is our servant, Raj. Don't let it use you rather, use it for your own benefit."

"I still can't believe I did it."

"I am so happy, you did it. This is truly nothing short of magical."

Aaliya couldn't stop herself and planted a kiss on his left cheek.

Chapter 15
CONFUSION OR CLARITY

Raj narrated the whole event to Monty, who made a mockery out of him.

"You are enjoying this to the fullest!" he said.

"It's not what you think. Aaliya knows Manasi, that's the only reason why I am in touch with her."

"Keep up the good work, man."

That evening, Raj went to the gym. He looked around for Aaliya but she was not there. He had just taken to the bench to start with some chest exercises, when he received a pat on his shoulder. He turned around to find Aaliya standing over him.

"Hi! Buddy, what's up?"

Raj asked her hesitantly, "Will you do some work for me?"

"What work?"

"I have written a letter to Manasi expressing all that I need to say to her, and it needs to be passed on to her."

"In the era of SMSes and E-mails, you are writing letters? Incredible. I'll applaud for you." She mimicked clapping her hands.

"I don't know her new mobile number and she has changed her email address too. Hence, the letter."

"And what you have written in that letter?"

"It's personal."

"It's personal? If it's so personal, why you don't give it to her yourself."

"Because, I am scared."

"What? Scared? She is your wife!" Aaliya exclaimed.

"She does not want to talk to me."

"Look if you are too afraid to talk to her, how can the problem ever be solved?"

"To solve the very problem, I have written the letter. Please understand. Give this letter to Manasi, somehow."

"And why should I do this?"

"Because you are my friend."

"What the fu*k? Friend? No, No, No…I am seriously fed up of this friendship concept. First you help friends then these 'friends', after their work is done, forget you as if they never knew you. I don't want to feel hurt. If you want me to help you, then you'll have to do me a favor."

"Anything, you ask."

"Consider it well."

"I have, tell me."

"Dinner at my favorite restaurant."

"Fine, at 8 o' clock, tomorrow."

Aaliya and Raj then went ahead to complete their workout for the day and Aaliya helped him with some other exercises.

The very next evening, Raj entered a fancy restaurant dressed smartly in a black shirt and black trousers. Ever since he had come to Mumbai, his sense of dressing had been upgraded too. The environment of the new city was slowly changing his personality for the better. Raj looked around for Aaliya and spotted a woman sitting alone two tables away, facing the other way. He walked upto her and called out gently, "Aaliya?"

The girl turned to look at him. To his surprise, it was Manasi. Raj was ecstatic. The universe has given him what he had desired for so long.

"Manasi? I am so glad to find you here!"

Manasi was shocked, and said, "Who invited you?"

"Aaliya."

"Oh, so this is her plan."

"Manasi, please forget what happened in the past. We can start a new life again."

"No. Don't even consider the possibility of that happening. What did you think? You would follow me all the way to Mumbai and I'd forget everything, that I would change? No. You are still a loser and nothing else, for me."

Manasi stood up to go.

"Manasi, please sit down. Everyone is staring us."

"I don't care…I am leaving," she said aloud as she turned to walk away from him.

Raj pleaded after her, "Manasi, please stay. Manasi… Manasi…I will do whatever you want. Manasi, I am changing myself for you…Manasi, please…Manasi."

She stopped in her tracks, turned and walked back to him. Challenging him, she said, "Raj, the day you become a hero from the zero that you are, I will come back to you myself." Saying this she left, while everyone at the restaurant had their eyes glued either on her leaving furiously or on him sitting dejectedly.

CHAPTER 16

THE MOMENT OF TRUTH

Raj was awfully depressed and everywhere he looked, he saw failure and loss staring back at him. The word Loser had stuck to his mind like a leech, sucking away his peace of mind. The word had become his identity. He was scribbling something on his tab, when Monty strode in humming a Bollywood song and found his friend in a sorry mood.

"Raj what are you doing?" He grabbed the tab from his hand to find 'Zero' scribbled on it.

"I thought you were watching porn. Whenever I feel upset, I watch 'BB ki vines' or listen to some derogatory songs or watch porn. Give me that tab."

He removes the middle line from "Z" and fixes it in the middle and rotated the alphabet by 90 degrees to make it into an "H".

"There is only a difference of one alphabet between Zero and Hero. What are you doing my friend? Your wife has challenged you. You understand that? You have to do something to prove your worth to her."

Raj, still hoping to get her back, said, "What should I do then?"

Monty suggests a lot of ridiculous options like becoming Arnold Schwarzenegger or Michael Jackson or Rajesh Khanna.

Raj bursted out laughing at his suggestions. Monty felt good for having altered his friend's mood a little.

"Let's do one thing. Let's think together. Think, think,

think."

Raj joined him in his adventure of thoughts, when suddenly something struck Monty.

"Idea! You run. You run, my friend. Your wife was angry with you because you couldn't catch the thief. You do one thing. You run. Think about it, if you win some running competition, there is a chance that your wife gets impressed and comes back."

Raj was reluctant with his idea, "How can you expect a man in his 30s to run?"

"What the hell you are saying? This is the only thing which everyone can do, right from a kid to a 105 years old Fuaja Singh. You forgot, you ran after Aaliya's auto for more than 10 kilometers and that too without any stomach pain. You run, my friend. You run."

"But which run?"

"The Marathon."

Raj did not feel as excited for the suggestion, "Who will run that much?"

Monty gave him options, "Who is asking you to run the full 42 kilometers? There are shorter 10 and 20 kilometer runs too. You might as well pick those to run at."

Raj made up his mind and decided to run.

Chapter 17

THANE MAYOR VARSHA MARATHON - 10 KMS RUN

Raj had never participated in a sports event before, either at school or at college. It was his first time getting involved in something as athletically challenging as a Marathon. He reached the event location well before time. Since Monty had no hopes from Raj, he thought it better to enjoy his sleep and go for his regular morning jog than to travel 25-30 kilometres from Juhu to Thane, get tired running 10 kilometers and then come back home somehow. It's easier to preach than to actually get involved in action.

The morning light was spreading quickly across the sky and a number of runners started flocking in. Raj overheard some of them stating their fastest timing to each other. One said that his best time was 75 minutes; another said that he didn't care for timing as he ran for the fun of it. Yet another enthusiast said that he was there for the first time and was not entirely confident about finishing the distance. Raj wondered what the run was all about and why had so many people, not only the residents of Mumbai, but also from far off places like Aurangabad, Surat, Ahmedabad, Bangalore, Hyderabad and even from New Delhi had come to participate in it. What was so special about this sport that so many people engaged in it just for the fun of participation? Raj was amused to see some government schools present there for participation too.

The run was organized by the Mayor of Thane, in association with the Maharashtra Athletic Federation. The son of the famous actor and director Mahesh Manjarekar had just arrived as the chief guest at the event. Raj could not remember his name as he had been a new entry to the Marathi Film Industry. The street was buzzing with runners and spectators. A tight security had been arranged by the Thane Police and a few NGOs and sports organizations gave their voluntary support too. Around 3000 runners had gathered to run the 10 kilometer stretch. The Mayor of Thane dropped the flag and the race began. Raj was in the first group and tried to stay within it while running. Since he wasn't acquainted with the route well, he decided to stay in the group as long as he could.

One of his fellow runners had painted his bald head and was running very well. His painted head captured Raj's attention and interest as he had written 'I am a Hero'. For the first time in his life, Raj saw someone who considered himself a Hero. One thought led to another and he was reminded of Monty showing him 'Hero' on his tab. A plethora of thoughts stringed one after the other housed in his mind and he loved how clearly he could focus and dissect them in his head while running. After about half the distance, the group grew smaller. Some runners from his group started accepting water bottles from the spectators' enroute, but he chose to focus on the rhythm of his body. As the distance to the finish line got shorter, the competition grew fierce. The man with the painted head started taking longer strides. It became hard for Raj to keep pace with him. His strides were shorter, thus he took more steps to cover the same distance, which meant that he had to infuse more energy into the run. Raj grabbed an energy drink from the next enroute table he spotted. It helped him for a little distance, but the lead runner was still paces ahead and was maintaining the distance.

Raj could hear the sound of a loudspeaker now, the last stretch of a kilometer had begun. Soon, Raj could see the 500 meters mark. Two options rose in his head; he could either secure a comfortable second position that day and try winning the next race at some other event, or he could try pushing all his energy to the limit and give a last attempt to win this competition. He chose the second option. There was no strategy anymore, no thinking and no calculation. All he had to do was to just believe in himself and know that he would be the winner. His pace picked up automatically, his heart started to beat faster, each muscle of his body seemed dedicated to make him sprint faster, the blood in his veins were carrying more oxygen to his heart and the body started to feel lighter. He was soon at par with the painted-head runner. They were less than 20 meters away from the finish line. With one final boost of energy, Raj lunged forward and crossed the finish line a step ahead of the man with the painted head.

He came to know that he had won only after he heard his jersey number being announced as the winner over the loudspeaker. People rushed towards him from all directions to congratulate and hug him, but he has escaped into some kind of a trance. His senses were on a different plane, where there were no sound, no noise; only feeling and more feeling. He knew that he had done it. The Mayor later awarded him with the Victory medal.

Sometimes, we don't know what we are capable of unless we try it for ourselves.

Chapter 18
THE MOTH GETS WINGS

Monty and Raj were riding to the stadium where Raj had started practicing his running after office hours. Monty suggested that he should take training from Aaliya.

Here Aaliya was more than happy to train Raj, as this gave her an opportunity to get closer to him. Aaliya searched for the best Marathon training programs over the internet. She finally chose a 16-week Marathon Training Plan.

16 week Marathon Training Plan

WEEK	MON	TUE	WED	THU	FRI	SAT	SUN
1	Rest	3 m run	4 m run	3 m run	Rest	5	Cross
2	Rest	3 m run	4 m run	3 m run	Rest	9	Cross
3	Rest	3 m run	5 m run	3 m run	Rest	10	Cross
4	Rest	3 m run	5 m run	3 m run	Rest	7	Cross
5	Rest	3 m run	6 m run	3 m run	Rest	12	Cross
6	Rest	3 m run	6 m run	3 m run	Rest	Rest	Half Marathon
7	Rest	3 m run	7 m run	4 m run	Rest	10	Cross
8	Rest	3 m run	7 m run	4 m run	Rest	15	Cross
9	Rest	4 m run	8 m run	4 m run	Rest	16	Cross
10	Rest	4 m run	8 m run	5 m run	Rest	12	Cross
11	Rest	4 m run	9 m run	5 m run	Rest	18	Cross
12	Rest	5 m run	9 m run	5 m run	Rest	14	Cross
13	Rest	5 m run	10 m run	5 m run	Rest	20	Cross
14	Rest	5 m run	8 m run	4 m run	Rest	12	Cross
15	Rest	4 m run	6 m run	3 m run	Rest	8	Cross
16	Rest	3 m run	4 m run	2 m run	Rest	Rest	Marathon

There was something more important than just pure running which was required and Aaliya had her mind set on that.

Aaliya took Raj to Matherun hills which were excellent for endurance training. It was a 7-day program, so Raj took leave from office for a week. Both of them stayed in the mountains at their respective camps.

Day 1: It was a bright sunny morning; Raj finished his morning trail run of 3 miles. After some rest and a protein diet, Aaliya took him to the Echo valley. It was a beautiful place enroute Garbett Point, and famous for the resounding echoes one could hear of their own voice there. Aaliya and Raj found a spot on a hillock beside the valley and stood there for a moment to enjoy the view.

Aaliya said, "Today we will practice affirmations."

Raj could remember having heard the word before, "Affirmations! I have heard about it but I don't know what it means in detail."

She explained, "Affirmation means to affirm oneself. Whatever we want in our life, we have to repeat it in our mind, continuously."

"Why?"

"Our mind works with the present. If we repeat one thing in our mind over and over again, our mind starts believing that it is true."

Raj was amused by the logic and said, "You mean to fool the sub-conscious by the conscious mind."

"Exactly, now look at the valley and take the feel in."

They turned towards the valley.

Raj asked, "How do I take the feel in?"

Aaliya explained by demonstrating, "Take deep breaths."

Raj took a deep breath and filled his lungs with fresh air.

"Raj, this is not the right way. Breathe with your stomach. Like this." She demonstrated again with hand gestures.

Raj took five deep breaths as Aaliya had instructed him and he could feel the difference.

Aaliya said, "Now say, you are the winner of this marathon."

Raj looked at her puzzled, “How can you predict the future?”

“Don’t think just say,” she insisted.

Raj kept quiet and turned his gaze back to the valley.

“Say, I am the winner of this marathon.”

“I am the winner of this marathon.”

As Raj spoke the sentence aloud, the echo sounded as if the whole valley stated Raj as the winner of the marathon. It was magical. Keeping up the mood and feel, Aaliya proposed another affirmation.

“Say, I am the fastest marathoner.”

“I am the fastest marathoner.”

“Say, I am the best.”

“I am the best.”

Aaliya then shouted with a quirk in her tone, “Say, I love Aaliya.”

Raj’s mind was still alert. He knew how to deal with her.

“I love…”, he stopped to assess Aaliya’s reaction and then proceeded to say, “I hate Aaliya.”

Aaliya realised his naughtiness and attacked him playfully. “What ‘I hate Aaliya’?”

Raj started running and Aaliya chased after him yelling, “You! Stop. I’ll see you.”

Day 2: Raj completed a 4 mile run through the Matherun forest. It was a beautiful experience for him to be so close to nature, especially while running through the greenwood. He felt as if the trees were speaking to him, while the air whistled through his ears and the sweet smell of wild flowers filled his senses. He wondered why man ran after a city life; true living resided there in the middle of the jungle.

Aaliya spread two mats on a rock facing towards the valley. Aaliya asked him to take his place on it and practice meditation.

Raj was curious and asked, "What is meditation?"

"Meditation is a practice where an individual operates or trains the mind or induces a mode of consciousness, either to realize some benefit or for the mind to simply acknowledge its contents without becoming identified with that content, or as an end in itself."

"Please elaborate; what you said sounds like a Wikipedia explanation."

"The term méditation refers to a broad variety of practices that includes techniques designed to promote relaxation, build internal energy or life force and develop compassion, love, patience, generosity and forgiveness. A particularly ambitious form of meditation aims at achieving an effortlessly sustained single-pointed concentration, which is meant to enable its practitioner to enjoy an indestructible sense of well-being while engaging in any life activity."

"Can we learn some such techniques?"

"Yes, today we will discuss the different techniques of Meditation. Broadly, there are as many as 23 meditation types, some of which are:

1. Buddhist Meditation (Zen Meditation) which includes Vipassana Meditation, Mindfulness Meditation and Loving Kindness Meditation (Metta),
2. Hindu Meditation (Vedic and Yogic) which includes Mantra Meditation (Om Meditation), Transcendental Meditation, Yoga Meditation, Self-Inquiry and 'I AM' méditation,
3. Chinese Meditation (Taoist Meditation) which includes Qigong (Chi Kung),
4. Christian Meditation, and
5. Guided Meditation"

"It seems that all religions have their respective forms of meditation."

"Correct, but all kinds of meditation are aimed at one single goal, which is to align our soul, heart and mind to the universal consciousness."

Raj thought deeply about what she was trying to say.

"What are you thinking?" Aaliya asked.

Raj opened himself to her and said, "Come on. Give me a hug."

"Are you sure?"

"Damn sure."

Aaliya went over to hug him tightly and felt for a moment that she had forgotten herself.

Loosening his grip, Raj proposed, "Will we not do meditation today?"

"We are currently engaged in the Loving Kindness Meditation together," Aaliya said, refusing to let go of Raj.

Raj smiled and her let her embrace him for as long as she wanted.

Day 3: It was a hot afternoon and sun burned down on them with full strength. Aaliya was waiting for Raj at the Garbett Point, which was situated opposite to the Matherun Hill Station. Tourists seldom went over to that side as it required them to walk at least 4-5 kilometres to reach the destination. The place was more popular with trekkers and served as a pit stop on the way down to Diksal waterfalls. It was a steep descent of at about 3 kilometers into the beautiful valley ahead that one could see from the Garbett Point. Raj soon joined her there.

"So, what is today's deal, trainer?"

"I want you to run from here to there." She pointed down the valley.

"There?"

"Hmmm."

Raj looked down at the valley and replied, "But it's

impossible to go there."

"Raj, nothing is impossible." Aaliya was all pumped up in her training mode.

Raj stressed further, "You can't even see all the way down. There is a trench there."

"Have you seen the trench yourself? Have you ever been down there? At least go and witness it for yourself. Perhaps you'll find a way."

Raj felt exasperated, "Are you a trainer or a devil?" he said.

Raj stepped ahead, fearing that it could be the last day of his life.

"Give me whatever names you wish. I will do everything possible to make you a splendid marathon horse," she said. "Calling me a Devil," she mumbled aside.

Raj slide down the steep path, losing his balance and almost fell into the deep gorge a meter ahead. Thanks to his running shoes, his feet regained a grip. Slowly and steadily, he looked around for a better way to descent into the valley. There were sharp rocks jutting out all across the steep declines. He made his way around them somehow and descended slowly. Aaliya watched him from the Garbett Point and was feeling proud. Raj finally touched a flat plateau, ran to the end of the plateau and came back. He now had to climb up the mountain, that too after having lost all his stamina during the descent and the run. It was the real test of his endurance. Climbing at an angle of almost 80 degrees seemed impossible from a distance but Raj decide to focus only on the step he was taking and the one after it. Following this strategy, he covered the entire distance in no time. What had seemed impossible a few minutes ago had become the reality of his present. Raj reached the top and Aaliya greeted him with a big hug and two kisses, one on each cheek. Offering him an energy drink, she took out a paper from her pocket.

"Raj, I want to share a poem with you."

"It's not the time to listen to a poem, let me rest a little, and then I can listen to it."

Aaliya didn't care what he said and started reading aloud,

Open your arms open your wings
Climb to the clouds and color them a new
Take light from the sun in your eyes
You are free to touch the sky
If you trust yourself
Break all the shackles
All the problems will vanish
Connect the unknown ways to reach the destination
Destroy the past with the present
Touch your own sky
Touch your dreams

-By Bhagesh RD

Day 4: It was early morning and sun was kissing the horizon. Aaliya entered Raj's tent. Raj was still sleeping. She found a place to sit beside him and looked at his tired and spend self.

She thought to herself, "Why I am helping this guy? He belongs to another woman. He is only using me and after he is done, he'll go back to his wife and I will be left alone because I am just a friend. I am in love with this married man. I shouldn't be. Why do I force myself on him to this extent? Aaliya, don't cross the line. Control yourself. Go back to basics. Yes, I have to go back to basics. I should find my own affirmations. I am a soul who has come here for human experiences. Every experience is created by my own self for the purpose of learning and knowing. I am an unconditional soul. Nothing will remain on earth besides these experiences. This is what I am here for; I shouldn't indulge in mindless calculations. I need to go by my instincts. Yes, I love this person lying next to me but I should never expect any love in return from him. That's me. That's Aaliya."

She felt a wave of goodness run through her. She looked at Raj's sleeping form again and bent down to look at him more closely. She inched ahead slowly and her lips touched his. She opened her eyes to see his face one more time, then got up and left the tent."

Raj woke up after sometime and searched for Aaliya outside the tents. He found her sitting beside a dying bonfire, sipping on coffee.

"Good morning," he greeted her.

"A very good morning, Champ."

"So what's in store for me today?"

"Today is rest day but a very important day for you to learn, or I should say to know."

"Know what?"

"Today, we will talk to the wind, trees, stones, sky, mountains, waterfalls, our body and everything else which our five senses can taste, see, touch, smell and hear."

"We are humans and these are the elements of nature. We cannot communicate."

Aaliya declares, "That's a wrong assessment, boss."

Raj confronts, "We have been taught this since childhood. How could it be wrong?"

"We accept whatever we are taught. We start believing without question anything."

Raj could see the point in her statement.

"We all are made up of energy which constitutes of these elements of fire, air, water and earth. We are as much a part of nature, as are the trees, stones, the sky, mountains, waterfalls and our body. We also know that similar energies attract one another. Thus when you believe or know that you are a friend to the wind, you can talk to it. Similarly, you can talk to any element of the Universe."

"We can talk to God too?"

"We all are our own Gods."

Raj contradicted her, "Now what's this? How can we be Gods?"

"Yes, we are. The mind cannot comprehend God but the soul can. A soul operates only on the level of feelings. So, feel everything."

"I can never bring myself to believe what you are saying, let's discuss some other topic."

Aaliya spontaneously said, "It will rain tonight."

Raj looked up at the sky. There were no clouds.

"No chance."

"And if it does?"

"Then you can demand anything from me and it shall be given."

Aaliya smiled at him as he had just uttered one of the most powerful statements of the universe. Aaliya opened her arms and looked to the sky as if it had already started raining and felt the rain drops on her face. Raj couldn't believe the girl's madness and went straight back to his tent to sleep.

It was dark already, by the time Raj woke up from a deep sleep. It was nearing dinner time. Aaliya had cooked some vegetables which she brought from a nearby village and also got their water bottles filled. Aaliya was eating her meal when he joined her.

"How was your sleep?"

"Dreamless."

"Good. That means you had a perfect deep-sleep."

Raj took a plate out of his bag, poured some vegetables

in a bowl and picked up some chapattis. As soon as he took the first bite, a drop fell on his face. An alarm went off in his mind. Within seconds, it started pouring heavily from the sky. Raj couldn't believe what was happening. He looked at Aaliya.

She smiled and said, "It's simple."

Raj rushed towards his tent with the plate of food in his hand. He remembered the promise he had given Aaliya, but hesitated in bringing it up for the fear that she could ask for anything.

The rain got more intense with each passing minute. The villagers in the valley could see that it was only raining over the mountain top but this was a usual phenomenon for them as Sahyadri ranges were prone to such kind of rainfall. Rain water from the mountain tops flowed down the slopes through naturally formed gutters and gullies. Raj's tent came in the way of one such ravine. Water started flooding into his tent, which he had to leave with all his belongings. A thought of entering Aaliya's tent to escape the downpour entered his mind, but the fear of the promise kept him from doing so. So, he remained standing in the open. Aaliya popped her head out of her tent out of curiosity, only to find Raj standing in the rain, getting soaked to the bone. She grabbed an umbrella and ran towards him.

"Are you mad? These rains will get you sick."

She grabbed his hands and pulled him into her tent. Raj was completely drenched. She gave him her towel to dry himself with and a pair of t-shirt and pants to change into.

As he was about to wear the pants, she said, "Stop."

Raj looked at her surprised.

"You have a promise to fulfill."

"Promise!"

"You promised me, remember?"

"Yes, what do you want from me?"

She wanted to say, Don't wear anything. I am going to remove my clothes too and then you can make love to me all night. But she said nothing.

Before she could utter a word, Raj quickly put on his pants.

"You can sleep in my tent but there is only one sleeping bag here. We'll have to adjust. It's big enough for both of us, I think."

"No, I will sleep beside you; you can take the sleeping bag all to yourself."

Aaliya slipped inside the bag and dozed off within minutes. Raj soon started feeling cold and his entire body shivered with it. He wanted to slip into the sleeping bag too, but his morals stopped him.

Aaliya woke up to the loud chattering of his teeth. Without opening her eyes, she slid open the zip of her sleeping bag and slowly extended one edge of the opening towards Raj. He had no choice but to accept the rescue of the sleeping bag. As he slipped into it, he felt enveloped by the heat that Aaliya's body had created inside. He checked whether she was asleep or not. She kept her eyes shut so that he wouldn't guess her awake. He ziped up the sleeping bag around himself slowly. Aaliya turned casually towards him. Raj could feel her breath on his neck. It was too dark inside the tent to see anything. She then slipped her arm around Raj. He tried to remove her hand but the lack of space inside the sleeping bag restricted all movement. Aaliya had the perfect opportunity. She pressed forward and brushed her lips onto his. Raj tried to escape but before he could move, her tongue had entered his mouth. Raj now knew that Aaliya was awake. He didn't participate in the kiss. Aaliya then whispered into his ears.

"I want to teach you what real love is."

"I know what love is."

"That might be your interpretation of love. I want to tell you mine."

"I am not interested."

"I still have a promise pending."

"I understand what you want but I am a married man."

"This night is ours and I want it entirely from you."

"It's not possible."

Aaliya hand moved towards his borrowed pants. She could feel the stiffness of his organ underneath.

"But your organ is ready for what it wants."

Raj removed her hand.

"You have to keep your promise."

"I am sorry. Don't ask me for it."

"Okay, you don't have to do anything, let me do what I want. Will that be a problem?"

Raj didn't utter a word as his body was now ruling his mind. Aaliya slide down and tasted Raj's manhood. He could feel the heat rising in waves through his whole body. Yet, he tried to restrict himself. Aaliya was going with the flow, following her instincts. She removed her pants and positioned herself upon his face. She had lost herself in the rhythm of her movements and tempted Raj to lick her.

"You call this love?"

"No, it's the activation of energies in our bodies."

"What energy?"

"It's activation of the Root Chakra."

"Chakra?"

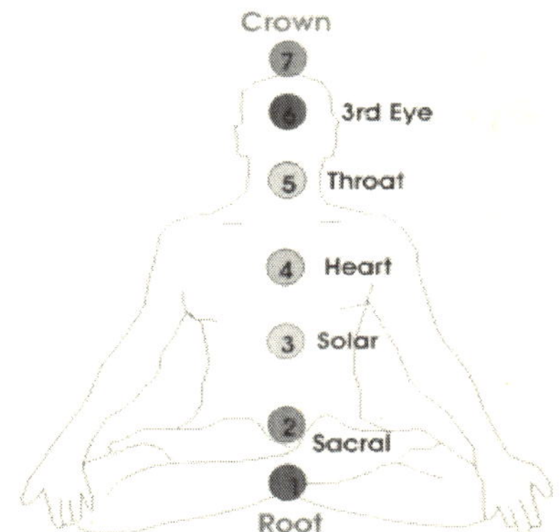

"Energy points. Let me do the job."

"What are you saying? I don't understand."

"There is nothing to understand, just go with the flow."

"I don't like this licking activity."

"Is that why Manasi left you."

"What the hell?" He pushed her aside. "Enough is enough."

Aaliya turned inside the sleeping bag to face him.

"Let me teach you how to make love. There are seven chakras in our body; Root, Sacral, Solar, Heart, Throat, the Third Eye and Crown Chakra. Root Chakra is where all the sexual energy resides and it is the most powerful energy center. Two beings can make perfect love only when they activate love arousing energies of the chakras in their body. A man who loses out in a few minutes is only having sex. Whereas, a man who understands the relationship between love and sexual energies, can make love to a woman the whole night. A woman's arousal takes time and she makes love with her whole body while a man makes love only with the one organ. Despite that, if a man understands his woman, he can make her have as many orgasms as he wants. Do you know, a woman can have up to 24 orgasms? Isn't it amazing? A man, however, can have only one. A man, who is in control of his senses, can achieve it by controlling the ejection."

"But that's not possible."

"Everything is possible in this universe. I can prove it to you."

"But…"

Before he could speak, Aaliya pressed her lips with his.

The temptation had overtaken Raj's senses, but Aaliya stopped him from entering her.

"Why do you stop me now?"

"First, get me aroused to the fullest, make me ready to accept you and then I will help you myself to get inside me."

"What should I do now?"

"Just go with the flow."

Raj kissed her breasts and then proceeded to kiss every inch of her body, soon Aaliya starts moaning with pleasure. The heat in the sleeping bag had risen to enormous proportions and their bodies started sweating. Sweat, while love-making, is an excellent sign. It opens all the pores of the body so the skin can breathe fully. One good love-making session is as good as a 5 kilometre run. When Aaliya was ready, she picked up Raj's organ and asked him to enter her. Raj asked her softly, "Is this your first time?"

"Yes. So be careful," she replied.

Raj, with his experience to direct him, entered her slowly.

"I love you."

When he heard those words from Aaliya, he was transported back to his Suhaag Raat with Manasi, when he had said "I love you" to his new wife while making love.

Aaliya suffered pain for a few seconds, which she endured gladly. Raj was at the summit of his activity, while Aaliya was on the verge of her first orgasm. She moaned aloud for the entire valley to hear. She smiled a smile that no one could see, not even Raj. After she came, Raj increased his speed of his thrusts and was about to eject, when Aaliya interrupted, "Stop champ, stop. Be calm. Save the energy for running. Don't let it come out of you. Detach yourself from the mind. Focus only on giving the love. The more you stroke me, the more you express your love for me, as it would then let me have one orgasm after another."

After a few minutes of stroking, Aaliya got arousal again and Raj pleasured her the whole night.

It stopped raining as soon as the night was past. Raj hadn't ejected at all the previous night. When they saw each other in the first light of the morning, their faces shone as if bright light was emitting from their own body. Raj couldn't believe that he had slept with Aaliya. Various thoughts start racing through his mind.

"Will she tell Manasi about all this? Oh yes, she will. This is exactly what she wanted. She wants me, but I want Manasi. What should I do now? How should I convince Aaliya to not tell her about this night? Will she ask anything in return? Will she blackmail me? What an error I have made? Foolish me. Stupid me. I am such a bastard. God help me."

While these thoughts were running through his mind, Aaliya came and said inadvertently, "Don't worry, it's our secret."

"I think four days of training in enough for now. I want to go back to Mumbai."

"I will join you. We can complete the last three days in Mumbai itself."

Raj slept throughout their cab journey back to Mumbai and avoided any conversation with her. Aaliya kept looking at him now and then. She smiled and said to herself, "Ask and it shall be given."

Chapter 19

SATARA HILL MARATHON

Raj didn't go to the gym for a whole week after that day, neither did Aaliya make the effort to contact him. The next weekend, the famous Guinness World Record holder 'Satara Hill Marathon' was going to be conducted. Monty and Raj decided to take two days and survey the track before the actual race. They took the rail route and reached Satara on Saturday morning. The track had a 10 kilometres ascent and 10 kilometres descent. It was, however, a delight to the eyes with beautiful scenery on both sides. One could see the Ajinkyatara Fort and the Pratapgarh Fort along the route, both made under the reign of Shivaji Maharaj. Vast water bodies could also be seen on either side. They moved further ahead to find themselves on the beautiful Kaas Plateau filled with yellow, white and purple flowers. They had lunch beside the Kaas lake and also got a chance to see the Thoseghar falls.

Sunday was the official day for the Satara Hill Marathon. That year, there were more than three thousand participants who had registered for the Half-Marathon. In a Half-Marathon a participant has to run a distance of 21.0975 kilometers, or 13 miles. Satara Hill Marathon was one of the toughest marathons of the world. The previous year's winner Imran was participating again that day at the marathon. That local boy had covered the distance in 1 hour and 14 minutes. The people of Satara were anxious to see whether the local boy will become the champion runner again or will they have a new Satara Hill Marathon winner. Every runner that had come to participate was pumped up with enthusiasm. The good news was that one could listen to the live commentary of the run on FM radio that year.

Monty was very excited and kept motivating Raj all morning. Imran's coach gave him some last-minute suggestions too. The race was about to begin and the countdown started. The race director Dr. Sandeep Kante flagged off the race at 6 A.M. and the race began. A horseman was running ahead of the runners. The whole atmosphere was filled with the slogans of Jai Bhawani and Jai Shivaji and why not, as the city of Satara was founded by the legendary warrior king Shrimant Chhatrapati Shivaji Raje Bhosle. Media persons had collected on either side of the tracks and were clicking pictures. The local people had collected on the side of the road to cheer up the runners. The entire Satara Administration, including the Police, Government organizations, NGOs, hotel conglomerates, etc. had come to motivate the participants.

Due to the bulk of runners on the track, there wasn't enough space for Raj to cross ahead and surge his speed. Imran had already taken the lead and was running in the front row while Raj was in the tenth row. The entire route echoed with music and dance. Some local schools had come to present the local music along with some dancers. The town of Satara seemed to be in a celebratory mood.

Courtesy the radio coverage, Aaliya and the other gym mates could listen to the live commentary of the run from Mumbai. Aaliya had enabled the speaker mode on her mobile phone.

In the beautiful valley of Satara, every runner was putting his best effort. The runners had now crossed the first kilometer. The enthusiasm of the runners was incredible. Every participant was challenged now and again by the high mountains of Satara. Imran was crossing the runners one after another and had reached ahead. The top elite group led by Imran had crossed the tunnel.

The top runners were maintaining a remarkable speed of about 3.5 kilometers per minute, which was incredible. Imran was in the first place; then came Abdul from Uttar Pradesh, Karim from West Bengal, Peter from Kerala and then Raj from Maharashtra in the fifth place. Imran had maintained a good speed all through and it seemed likely that he would win this year too.

A reporter from Kaas Plateau reported that Imran was leading, with Karim in the second position and Raj as the third.

Back at the gym in Bombay, Aaliya exclaimed with joy, "Raj is in the third place!"

The runners had reached the half point. Imran was leading and Raj was following him. "Unbelievable, this man Raj has crossed Imran," another reporter exclaimed. The distance between Raj and Imran increased with each passing second. Raj was running with a steady speed, while Imran appeared to grow a little tired. Raj, maintaining his speed, had left the group behind.

A couplet by the poet Vidyasagar Singh needs special mention at this point for this brave man.

Those who overcome obstacles to accomplish their purpose have got real strength,

While those who lose a winning bet, suffer from a lack of courage and bravado.

(KATHINAIYON KO PAAR KARKE,
MANZIL WOHI PATE HAIN,
JEENAMEIN DUM HOTA HAI,
JETI HUI BAAZI KO,

WOH HAAR JAATE HAIN,
JINAMEIN HAUSLA KUM HOTA HAI.)

The 17 kilometers mark was only a few paces ahead. Raj was running at an unbelievable pace. Imran was still in the second place behind him.

Raj crossed a pole on which a loudspeaker was blaring, "Raj is leading! Will Imran lose? Who is going to be the winner and who, the loser?"

As soon as the word loser fell on his ears, his past came rushing in front of his eyes, as if it was the present. The haunting words of Manasi started to echo in his head.

"Stupid loser. I hate him. A person who can't even catch a thief. How can I spend my entire life with him? I can't live a life of compromise. You are a loser. I am trapped in this marriage. It's better to marry someone else then to adjust with you. Why don't you leave me? Stupid loser. I hate him. I hate him. I hate him."

Raj's mind was hacked by the words of Manasi. His sub-conscious mind pulled out every single memory of his moments of vulnerability and displayed it in front of his eyes. An ominous feeling enveloped him and forced him into inaction.

The radio commentary announced, "Where is Raj? He is not to be found anywhere. It appears that the last year's winner Imran will sweep the title yet again."

"Raj has vanished," Monty exclaimed, at the finish line.

Everyone was in shock, including Aaliya and the gym mates.

Taking the golden opportunity for himself, Sam commented, "A loser is always a loser."

Aaliya switched off the mobile and everyone who had gathered around her to listen to the commentary went back to their exercise machines.

Imran, the champion from the previous year, won the Satara Hill Marathon again. Monty waited for an announcement about Raj but there was none. He went upto the race director to enquire about Raj but he denied any information on him. Monty borrowed a bike from the organisers and left in search of Raj. Three kilometers ahead, he found Raj sitting on a rock facing the valley. His eyes were cast down and body bent in dejection.

Monty approached him and spoke, “Her memories have defeated you once again.”

Chapter 20

DEPRESSION IS THE DEATH OF SOUL

Raj had not spoken to Aaliya after that night. She tried to reach him over his mobile, but he did not respond. She did not even know where he lived in the city. Aaliya was curious about the reason for his failure. She knew that an introverted guy like Raj would never share his innermost feelings with anyone. Aaliya called the gym to get his address. The receptionist told her that Raj had registered with his office address. She then called his office for his address but Mr. Kamat refused to oblige as the office rules stated that no personal record could be shared with a third party. Aaliya was brainstorming over how to reach him, when an idea struck her. She put his number on a mobile tracker, which showed her his exact location. Aaliya followed the address and reached the terrace of his building, where she finally found him.

"Raj…what…have you gone mad? You haven't come to the gym for days. You are not responding to my calls and messages. What has happened? I am asking you something? Why are you so depressed? You should be happy. You should be happy that you were leading right up to 18 kilometers. Think, if marathon had only been up to 18 kilometers, you'd be the winner. You would have been the champion. Look Raj, you only need more practice. When you practice, you'd be able to win not just the 21 kilometers half-marathon, but also the 42 kilometers full marathon."

"I couldn't even run the 21 kilometers, how do you expect

me to run double that distance? For you, everything is magic. Just think and it gets realized."

"Why do you not understand? Remember how difficult it was for you to run earlier? You thought it was impossible to run even ten kilometers. But now, your stamina has increased manifold. 21 kilometers is child's play for you now. You need only to make up your mind. I guarantee, that you can definitely win a 42 kilometers marathon."

"I know you are a motivator and love to give lectures like this. Sometimes I wonder if you are a descendant of Napoleon. You've removed the word 'Impossible' from your dictionary."

"Yes I have."

"I don't trust myself all that much. But why do you trust me more than I do myself?"

"Raj, there is no reason for me to not have trust in you… and I know that once a man decides to achieve something, he definitely achieves it. I have always been this positive from childhood and now I want you to become this positive too."

Just then, Monty entered with two cups of tea, one each for Raj and himself. He hadn't expected to find another guest, however, he recognised her as soon as he saw her.

"Now I understand where my friend gets all his confidence from." Monty said and turned to Aaliya. "You are Aaliya?"

Aaliya responded, "How do you know?"

"He talks about you all the time."

"Really!?" She couldn't believe it.

Raj didn't want to participate in that discussion and left their company without saying a word.

"Where are you going buddy?" Monty asked.

Raj didn't respond.

"To his sorrow den," Aaliya told him.

"Sorrow den?"

"He loves to be in sorrow because that way he feels himself closer to Manasi."

"Yes, I know he has been living in a fantasy world, but he admires you."

"I am just a friend for him."

"Aaliya, I believe he needs you because he has changed a lot since your training days at Matherun."

"Changed?"

"I see signs of positivity in him. Go and get him."

Monty stayed on the terrace enjoying the beautiful sunset, While Aaliya followed Raj downstairs and entered his room. Raj was lying on his stomach on the bed. Aaliya found this as an excellent opportunity to jump on him.

"Champ, I had actually brought Manasi's letter for you."

This caught his attention. He turned around to look at her.

"Manasi's letter?"

"But since your mood is off, you probably won't read it. I should leave."

"No give the letter to me."

Aaliya started playing with the letter. He tried to grab it but she dodged each time.

"You want this letter? Then take it. Take it. Are you sure you really need it? If you do, then you'll have to give me something in return."

"Not again."

"Promise or I am going."

"What do you want?"

"I want you to come back to the gym."

"I will think about it."

"No thinking, just promise me."

"Okay, I promise. Give me the letter now."

Raj snatched the letter and started reading it.

"Dear Raj,

Congratulations that you participated in the Half Marathon. What happened between us is history. I wish that you run the 42 kilometers full marathon too."

Raj looked towards Aaliya, blushing and glowing with a wide smile.

"Aaliya, Manasi wants me to run the 42 kilometers marathon too."

"That's just great. When I asked you for the same thing, you declined, but when Manasi wants it, you accept without thinking. This is unfair. Do we not have any relation at all?"

"She is my wife."

"And I am just a friend."

Raj kept quiet.

"I am sorry for that night, Aaliya."

"Don't apologise for it. It was the most beautiful moment of my life."

Raj felt that it was better to remain silent.

"You got your wife's letter. Now will you dress up and come to the gym with me."

Raj put on his track suit and left the house with Aaliya.

CHAPTER 21

LION IS OUT FROM DEN

All the gym members watched Aaliya and Raj enter the gym together. Sam and his friends were working out on different machines. Sam hadn't liked Raj since the first day he saw him and his closeness to Aaliya always bothered him. Aaliya advised Raj to start with cycling. Raj took the empty bicycle and started pedaling. Sam couldn't contain himself and commented, "Here comes the shameless."

Aaliya understood right away who Sam was targeting.

She warned him, "You do your work."

Sam spoke to his friends, "There are lots of stupid people in this world. They have the confidence to show up even after losing. Bloody losers!"

Aaliya couldn't contain herself and yelled, "How dare you? Who are you to say this?"

"Aaliya, mind your language."

"He ran 18 kilometers in just one hour. You can't even run for 5 minutes continuously on the treadmill and you are comparing yourself with him."

"Yes friends, this guy called Raj has done a great work."

Raj tried to hold Aaliya back.

Aaliya spoke to Raj, "Leave me, let me deal with him."

Sam continued to remark, "He didn't even come last amongst 3000 runners."

The whole gym laughed with Sam. Encouraged by the response of his friends, Sam started chanting loudly and the others joined in.

"Loser. Loser. Loser."

The whole gym echoed with one word – LOSER. Aaliya couldn't restrain herself any longer. She lurched forward towards Sam and gave him a blinding blow to his face. Boom.

Sam fell flat on the ground. His hand reached up to check his face. He found blood oozing out of his nose. The receptionist summoned the gym manager who came rushing in.

He shouted aloud, "What the hell is going on here?"

Aaliya, still angry at Sam, threatened him, "You meet me outside the gym. I will make sure you understand or I'll change my name."

Without caring for the Manager's presence, Sam responded, "I will take revenge for this blood."

The Manager had to intervene. He commanded, "Silence! You should be ashamed. You all are fighting like people in the street. Go to your respective positions and resume your exercise."

Raj got the chance to console Aaliya. "Why did you get so angry?" he asked.

"He called you a loser."

Meanwhile, the Gym Manager talked to Sam.

"If someone from our gym participated or wants to participate in a marathon, then instead of supporting him you are making fun of him. You should be ashamed of yourself. I want you to apologise to Raj."

"I am sorry, Raj," Sam said and came forward to shake hands with Raj and Aaliya. Everyone else applauded to appreciate the peace between them.

After the workout, Raj and Aaliya walked back to her house. Aaliya was still upset. Raj wanted to speak to her but maintained his silence. They reached her building and she continued to walk inside. Raj looked at her go.

He felt something and shouted, "Aaliya."

She stopped and turned. Raj walked up to her and gave

her a hug.

"Thank you," he said softly.

In his arms, Aaliya proposed, "My parents will come late tonight, we have two hours."

Raj smiled and released her.

"You never miss a chance."

Aaliya smiled, "You are worth it."

"Good night, Aaliya."

Aaliya didn't say a word and watched him go.

Chapter 22
A CHALLENGE IS A CHALLENGE

Raj couldn't fall sleep as his mind kept repeating the incident at the gym over and over again in his head.

"He didn't even come last in 3000 runners."

He couldn't sleep the entire night. It was 3 A.M. and the time for him to go running. It was the best time for runners to practice in a city like Mumbai, as the roads were all empty. Between 2 and 5 in the morning was the only time when the city slept and not one soul could be seen awake on the road. Raj started his run and the anger and insult from the day's incident gave his pace an extra boost. The words and thoughts of disgrace were actually working in his favor. The extra push that he needed for the run was coming from the memory of those insults, shame and disaster. The first 21 kilometres were not so hard for Raj as he had the experience and stamina for it. But as the distance started to escalate, he started to face certain physical injuries. His armpits became bloody red as his arms were constantly rubbing against it. Both his nipples developed red rashes around them. An acidic liquid started flowing from his anus which hurted his buttocks movements. His eyes had become red as the sweat from his head trickled directly into them making his vision difficult. His body was dehydrated as all the fluids of the body had drained out. A strange head ache started to pick up throbbing at his temples. The sound of his heartbeat was so strong that even a passer-by could easily hear it. His socks were drenched with sweat and the running shoes filled with sweaty water. Raj could see the salt emerging from his skin, accumulate over his arms. This salt and the sweat hurt his skin badly. Despite such physical strain, Raj continued to run. He checked the running tracker app on his mobile which showed that 32 kilometres had been covered. Soon, his body felt a strong wave of fatigue. It wanted to stop Raj from running, but the insult and shame which he had faced at the gym kept him going. He didn't want to be known as a loser any more. Each step now became a struggle as his body had already given up. His brain was constantly sending signals to stop. But some different kind of energy was coming from within him, which asked him to continue. His inner self knew that this phase would be over soon. He continued on with the same pace. Endurance is the true word that explains the reality of Raj at that moment. Many a times, we undergo such a situation, in order to understand the real meaning of it. This moment of fighting with himself was a defining moment in his life. Moreover, Manasi had asked him to run a full marathon, while Aaliya had full surveillance on him. This constant fight with the mind and body had caused him to connect with his soul. He was in a state of trance, not knowing anything. Everything had become nothing. The reality around him had distilled to a big zero for his mind or body to perceive or understand. In that moment, he was free from all pain, desire, ego and success. He was running and running. A sudden ring of the phone brought him back to the present world of body and mind. He picked up the call, it was Monty.

"Raj, where are you?"

"I just finished my first 42 kilometers, I guess. Wait, let me check."

Raj opened his tracking app on the phone to check his distance and timing. His eyes shone bright as he told Monty,

"I ran 42 kilometers today in just 2 hours and 42 minutes, my friend."

"I can't believe it. This is incredible!"

Raj disconnected the call and dialed Aaliya. Aaliya picked up at the first ring.

"This is the first time you've called me, you know? There must be something really special. Did Manasi call you?"

"No, it's not Manasi."

"Then? What could have made you so happy?"

"Aaliya, I just completed a full marathon."

Aaliya squealed with joy and stood up on her bed.

"What are you saying?"

"Yes, Aaliya. I did it."

"I love you, my champion."

Raj was about to repeat the words back to her but controlled himself and disconnected the call. He looked towards the sky with gratitude, thanking the entire universe for what he has been able to achieve.

CHAPTER 23

WHEN THE SUN SHINES, DARKNESS HAS TO VANISH

During the office break one day, Rokade and Monty went to get some cold drink. Rokade had to share some news with Monty and decided to reveal it to him in person, on the pretext of a drinks break. Rokade siped on the cold drink and told Monty the good news.

"Monty, I am recommending your name for the Mauritius Business Conference."

"Thank you so much, sir." Monty was excited about the sudden offer of travel. "Sir, there is one more good news."

"Another good news?"

"Raj completed 42 kilometers in just 2 hours and 42 minutes."

"What are you saying, Monty? If I am correct, the world record for a full marathon is 2 hours and 3 minutes. I think this boy deserves world class training."

"Sir, he runs the whole day. What more could he need?"

"You don't know. People do all sorts of training for marathons, like Chi Training, Sand training, etc."

These terms were unheard of by Monty, hence his curiosity escalated.

"What did you say, sir? Chi, Sand…ch…I could not understand."

Rokade tried to explain, "Chi training, sand training, mountain training…there are various types of trainings for long distance running."

A doubt popped up in Monty's mind and he asked, "Sir,

but are these trainings available in India?"

A good question should always be followed by an excellent answer.

"I am sure they are in Mauritius."

As fortune favors the brave, Aaliya had gotten in touch with an international marathoner who, by good chance, was right there in Mauritius. Her name was Samantha and she had come to Mauritius for a vacation. Initially on e-mail, she refused to train Raj but Aaliya called her up on her personal number and requested again. Who could refuse the persistent Aaliya?

Chapter 24
UNIVERSE OPENS UP

Monty booked a flight for Raj at a discounted rate as he had close connections with the official photographer of Mauritius airlines. His name was Sachin Sagar, who gave him the discount coupons. Raj was curious, but full of questions at the same time, as to what he was supposed to do next. His stay was arranged at a beautiful resort near Flic-en-Flac. Mauritius, an island nation in the Indian Ocean, is known for its beaches, lagoons and reefs.

Whenever one travels out of the country for the first time, one tends to invest in a lot of research about the country and its people, out of curiosity and to a certain extent a fear of the unknown. Raj was pleased to find out that most of Mauritius' residents, except the French people, could speak either Hindi or Bhojpuri. It was an amusing, yet proud moment for Raj when he heard a Bhojpuri radio channel playing in the cab that he took to meet Samantha.

Samantha was an international marathoner who had won medals at many International Marathons like the Hong Kong International Marathon, Singapore International Marathon, Dubai International Marathon, Istanbul International Marathon, Berlin International Marathon, London International Marathon and many more. Raj has already googled and researched her profile online. After a short journey, he arrived at the Pereybere beach near Grand Bay where he was to meet her. He paid the cab in Euros. His mind automatically got busy converting the amount into

Indian Rupees and the expense surprised him out of his wits.

Raj was waiting for Samantha on a rock beside the beach when his phone started to ring. It was Aaliya.

"Hi, Champ! Did you meet Samantha yet?"

"I am waiting for her right now."

"Did you take your protein shakes and the diet that I had referred?"

"Yes, I had two rotis and 5 egg whites with one yolk as my first meal. Then after the morning run, I had one scoop of protein with slim milk and a banana to recover."

"Excellent. Take care of yourself and do as she recommends. And remember, she is a beautiful French girl, so be in control of your wandering eye. Be professional with her."

Raj laughed inwardly at Aaliya's fear, one that all girls have with respect to their boyfriends or husbands, when a far more beautiful woman is involved.

"I am here for training." Raj said, almost feeling Aaliya smile through the phone in response.

"Your mobile bill will shoot, let's disconnect now."

Aaliya did not want to disconnect. "I miss you," she said.

She was hoping for the same reply from Raj but he kept quiet. In her heart she knew well that she was second and would always remain second for Raj. Before she disconnected the call, she kissed her phone loud enough for Raj to hear.

Samantha had still not arrived. Raj was mesmerized by the beauty of the beach, the wonderful combination of colours all around him, that no painter could reproduce on his color board. Raj was interrupted by another phone call, which he assumed would be Samantha, but it was Monty.

"If you get a chance with her, don't back out," he said as soon as Raj picked up call.

"What do you mean?"

"Blond hair, beautiful skin, great height and an alluring face. Your trainer has all the qualities."

"How do you know?"

"I checked her Facebook profile. She looks great in a bikini."

Raj suddenly noticed a girl coming out of the water on the beach. It looked as if a mermaid was emerging out of the ocean. She wore a beautiful aquamarine bikini and her lips broke into a tender smile when she saw Raj looking at her. Raj guessed that this woman must be Samantha. She walked straight up to Raj, looking wet and wild. Raj disconnected Monty's call and diverted all his attention to her.

"Hi! I am Samantha," she greeted him with her hand extended towards him.

"I am Raj. Nice to meet you, Samantha," he said, taking her hand.

"Are you ready for the singing?" she asked.

Raj asked puzzled, "Singing?"

"Yes, my training will make your bones sing...Ooh, aah, ouch," she smirked.

"Ooh...aah...ouch." Raj repeated after her, smiling.

"Running is not a funny business. I will make you understand this once your training starts, which is from tomorrow."

"I am really grateful to have you as my trainer."

Both of them sat on the rock where she had found him.

"All of us need someone to guide us. I underwent a lot of training as well from the world's best marathoners."

Aaliya's face flashed across Raj's mind, how she guided him to continue the purpose of his life.

"What is the most important thing one needs to become a winner?"

"Visualization."

Raj kept quiet so that she may continue.

"You need to visualise, create pictures in your mind and see them happening. For example, if you want to win the International Marathon, you create a mental picture of yourself standing at the podium with a gold medal around your neck and flowers in your hand."

"It sounds a little illogical."

"Not all things that exist in this world function on logic. Don't let your mind be bothered by that aspect."

"Is there a way to shut up that part of my mind?"

"Yes, of course. Press your right nostril with your right hand and take deep breaths. This will activate the right side of your brain which is the creative centre and is linked to our sub-conscious mind. Whatever information you send to your sub-conscious mind, is what will happen with you."

"The other athletes must also indulge in this activity though. What happens then?"

"Yes, we all do. However, the person who does it first and has the desire and capability to win the most, attains the first place. Another important thing is that your sub-conscious mind must send the message to the super conscious mind, which we call God or the Universe."

"Conscious mind to the sub-conscious mind and further to the super-conscious mind," Raj repeated.

"You got that right. Now close your eyes and feel as if you are standing at the winner's podium. Everyone is looking at you and they are proud of you. You smell the flowers in your hand. Feel the fatigue you have achieved after the run. Look at the photographers clicking pictures of you. Absorb the feeling of being the world's inspiration."

The activity felt magical to Raj. He remembered the affirmations technique that Aaliya had taught him. He concluded in his mind that visualization was a step risen from affirmation itself.

The next day, he started early in the morning as he had to reach Gris Gris beach where Samantha was going to meet him. Raj ran the entire distance from Flic-en-flac to the Gris Gris beach. It crossed a good part of the island, from west to south, passing through beautiful hills, forests and open lands, all as beautiful as he had often seen in Bollywood films.

Gris Gris beach was a tourist site which offered the visitors a magnificent view of the sea from the cliff tops. This part of the island was not surrounded by coral reefs which causes the waves to crash with full force against the daunting cliffside, causing the water to splash thunderously against it. Beside the beach, there was a small garden which offered a space for one to relax while enjoying the view of the sea, the waves and the cliff-side. A narrow trail from the garden led down to a small beach, where one could admire the view of the sea up-close.

Raj walked down the trail and reached 'Roche Qui Pleure' which offered a most spectacular view of the waves crashing against the flanks of the cliff, giving an impression that the cliff side was weeping.

Raj found Samantha waiting for him there.

"How was the run?" she asked.

"Beautiful."

"You seem to be enjoying Mauritius. This island has the best sand to practice running. It will help train your thighs and calf muscles."

"Flic-en-flac has a long shore line. I will go for it."

"Brilliant. Today we are going to learn about 'Chi Running.'"

"Sounds interesting…what's it about?"

"Chi running is all about the forces of nature, the force of gravity, and the force of approaching the ground."

"What do you mean?"

"First you must maintain a 'posture' like this." She stood in front of him facing the water crashing against the rocks and demonstrated the correct posture for running.

"Then comes the 'full feet landing,'" she continued. "Next is 'lean forward', after which you need a 'right knee bend' and finally a 'knee lift'. Your arms must swing to the rear like the pedals of a bicycle. All these things will increase your energy and efficiency, while escalating your speed and reducing stress and the chances of injury."

Raj remarked, "Techniques do play a significant role in enhancing a runner's endurance."

"That's exactly what I am teaching you."

Both of them discussed the various aspects of running at length. Samantha enjoyed training Raj as he did not bother her with too many questions; he simply followed her instructions. Every guru wants an obedient disciple. After the training session, things became a little informal. Samantha started discussing her personal life and how it got disrupted when her boyfriend left her for another woman. Raj could only empathise with her. Raj had the impulse to share his own life's details but he stopped himself. Soon, Samantha got a call from her driver. She was heading to Port Louis and offered to drop Raj at Flic-en-Flac on the way in her brand new red Ferrari. While on the way, Raj asked her how she came to own the beautiful Ferrari. She told him that it was given to her by a sponsor. Raj was amused and wondered what all an athlete could gain from the beautiful sport of running. Raj was dropped off at his resort and he watched the beautiful Ferrari zoom away.

Another day was about to start and Raj made his way to the Belle Mare Beach on the east coast of Mauritius, which was a great spot for scuba diving and swimming. Samantha had decided to give Raj an experience of scuba diving as a method in training for breath regulation. The better one can regulate one's breathing, the better one can run. A boat was waiting for Raj at the pier. He could see Samantha on the deck in an orange bikini. With one of the best figures in the world, she looked great; strong muscular thighs, hard bust, chiseled arms, a long neck, perfect curves and a flat abdomen.

Samantha handed him the scuba gear, which included a mask, snorkel, fins, BCD (Buoyancy Control Devices), weight system, regulator, SPG (Submersible Pressure Gauge), a dive computer, a dive watch, a dive knife, a dive light, scuba gear bags, wet suits and dry suits, the scuba bank and the side mount and then briefed him about all the equipments. Samantha was a certified scuba diver from PADI (Professional Association of Diving Instructors), which is the world's leading scuba diver training organization.

After an initial demonstration, both of them were ready to dive into the water. As soon as they reached about 5 meters under, a sudden pain shot through Raj's temples and he felt as if his head would explode with the pressure. Samantha understood his anguish and immediately gestured at him to air tight his nose with his fingers and pop his ears by blowing hard. It was difficult for Raj to understand so she demonstrated it for him to follow. Soon, his headache was gone. As they reached 10 meters under, a pair of white-tipped sharks crossed past them. An electric current through Raj's body as he had never seen full grown sharks up-close. A few meters ahead, there was a sea turtle and a Moray eel and a colony of oysters. What Raj liked best however, was to swim amongst hundreds and thousands of small yellow fish that appeared to enjoy his company rather than being afraid.

Raj was so lost in the beautiful world under water that he almost forgot his way. He looked for Samantha all around but she was nowhere to be seen. A wave of panic rushed through his brain and he decided to head straight for the surface. Before he could start deflating, he felt a pat on his head. He turned his head up to find Samantha right above him and he felt a quick relief spreading through him.

As they proceed on, they saw a big Mantha Ray, which had flippers as big as a jumbo jet's wings. Samantha smiled at Raj and signalled at him to monitor his dive watch. Raj looked at the watch which indicated that they had been under water for about 45 minutes. Samantha checked Raj's oxygen tank which indicated that he could only stay underwater for nine more minutes. She deflated Raj's as well as her own BCD and both of them drifted up towards the surface. As soon as their heads popped out of the water, she whistled at the boatman to come to pick them up. While the boat was on the way, Samantha noticed that Raj's eyes were wet.

"The dive really moved you, huh?" she asked gently.

"There are so many different worlds in this universe and we are free to choose our own."

Samantha couldn't resist hugging him and threw her arms around his neck.

The boat arrived and took them over to the shore. Raj was quiet the entire journey back and Samantha looked on quietly at his deep sombreness and serenity.

She dropped him off at the resort but her mind was now captured by him. Never before had she met a person who was so calm, pure and genuine as he was. Even her beauty had no effect on him. Samantha couldn't resist the temptation and decided on a different plan.

The next morning, Raj was taking rest at his room after an hour of swimming in the open sea, when a knock at his door woke him. He was pleasantly surprised to find Samantha at the door.

"Weren't we supposed to meet at Rochester falls in the evening?"

"There is a change of plans. Today will be a rest day."

"Rest day? But I went for an hour-long swim just this morning."

"Running daily can strain your body muscles in a bad way. You need to give it a rest time to time, at least once a week. During this rest, it is best to massage our body and fortunately for you, I have brought with me the world's best massage oils."

She brought forth a bottle, the label on which read 'Aloe Vera Distill Virgin Sesame Oil'.

"Massaging can help relax and rejuvenate the body very quickly. It helps enhance the blood circulation throughout the body which makes your bones and muscles much stronger. Good blood circulation and the nutrients in the massage oils ensure a smoother and softer skin too."

Raj's skin has tanned during the training program. The rich chocolate color of his skin however, looked all the more erotic and appealing to Samantha. She asked him to remove the t-shirt and lie on his stomach and proceeded to pour oil into her left palm and applied it onto Raj's toned back.

"You know, runners love getting these body massages. Not only does it feel great, but also brings about a speedy recovery, reduces muscles soreness and facilitates the healing of injuries. There are various kinds of massages, but the ones I like most are Active Release Massage, Deep Tissue Massage, Trigger Point Massage and my favorite, Swedish massage.

Swedish massage involves long, flowing strokes with varying pressures, though usually light, to release muscle tension and increase the blood flow. Swedish massage is the best to indulge in before big competitions, or as a recovery practice after intense workouts. The lighter, relaxing strokes help relieve stress and muscle tension without damaging the muscles, which is important if you have a big race coming up. A Swedish massage right before a race, especially if you're coming off a hard week of training, can help you re-energize, relax and build the confidence in your ability to run fast."

Samantha enjoyed caressing his body as his back muscles had toughened due to the intense training that he had undergone. The rich tan color of his skin was a major trigger for Samantha and she couldn't resist her impulses anymore. Raj, on the other hand, lay comfortably, completely unaware of what was going through Samantha's mind. She asked him to turn over and placed her hands gently on his chest. Her hands started to massage down his chest and moves to his belly. She was giving all the right signals but no response came from his side. Out of desperation, she kissed his lips. Raj opened his eyes astonished and saw her beautiful face hovering right above hers. Without wasting a second more, he shoved himself aside. "I am sorry," he said.

Samantha finally revealed what she felt in her heart, "I have started liking you."

"But I like someone else."

Tears came to her eyes but she controlled herself, "Who is the lucky girl?"

"My wife."

"You are a married man?"

"Yes, I am."

"Then how is Aaliya related to you."

"She is just a friend."

"The way she convinced me to train you, it sounded as if she was interested in you."

"I know that."

Samantha picked up the cap of the bottle and started screwing it down. "I am sorry for the kiss," she said.

Raj kept his eyes cast down as Samantha packed up and left the room. The next day, Raj called Monty up and asked him to prepone his flight. A day after, he landed back in Mumbai. He found Aaliya waiting for him at the arrivals gate of the airport. She came running to him as a child runs to meet his parents after school and enveloped him in a rib-crushing hug. Raj looked at her and felt deep passion and happiness radiating from her smile.

CHAPTER 25
ATTACK AND DEFENCE

After the intensive training program with one of the world's best marathoners, Raj continued the routine run from home to his office.

Kamini, the hot girl at office, was bored with her work and decided to indulge in a bit of mischief. She rose from her chair and approached Monty, but he was busy with his work. Her attention was then caught by Raj's sleeping form at his desk. He was taking a nap in the office. She immediately went straight to Mr. Kamat and complained, "Sir, Raj is sleeping at his work station."

"What? You go and sit at your own seat."

Kamini walked back to her seat smiling, as she knew some major drama was about to unfold.

Kamat walked up to Raj's desk and found him sleeping, as Kamini had told him. Kamat loudly tapped over his desk thrice.

"Mister Raj," he bellowed.

Raj woke up with a shock. He hadn't realised when he drifted off at his desk. The sound attracted the attention of all the other employees at office, who turned around at their respective seats to look at Raj and Mr. Kamat.

"This is an office, not your bedroom," he yelled.

"Sorry, sir."

"What sorry?"

Monty interrupted, "Sir, you should forgive him."

"It'll be in your best interest to keep work and friendship

separate, Monty." Kamat then shouted, "Lallan Singh!"

Lallan came rushing in towards them.

"Yes, sir."

"Bring the files from cupboard number three."

Lallan scurried away towards the cupboards.

Kamat anger was still not at an end, as he continued fuming, "You think yourself a hero?"

Lallan Singh entered again with a huge pile of files in his arms and stood beside Mr. Kamat.

"What are you looking at? Put the files down."

Raj looked at the pile perplexed, "Sir, so many files?"

Kamat's rage had now reached its peak.

"I want the work completed in two days," he barked at him.

Monty had to interfere, seeing that the angry Mr. Kamat was about to slaughter his friend. "Sir, this amount of work is not possible even in 15 days," he said, trying to persuade him against his decision.

"Do late sittings then," Kamat suggested. "I don't care how you do it, I just want the work done by tomorrow evening. Do you understand?"

After the demon had unloaded his vileness onto Raj, it was time for the angel to come rescue him. Mr. Rokade, who had been busy in a meeting with the CEO, exited the boss's office just then and felt negatively charged environment first-hand.

Rokade walked up to them and asked, "Kamat Sir, why you are so disturbed?"

Kamat kept quiet, so Rokade turned his gaze towards Raj.

"Raj, what happened?" he asked.

Before Raj could say anything, Kamat exposed Raj's folly.

"He was sleeping?"

Rokade understood Raj's situation immediately. "Oho, so what Kamat sir? Why you are after the poor boy? You know this boy comes to office by running 20 kilometers in the morning and runs the same distance back home after his work is complete. Anyone would get tired under such circumstances, Mr. Kamat. He only took a nap, it's no big deal."

Kamat countered by saying, "The energy he puts into running, had he put the same in his work, he would have reached great heights by now."

Rokade took Raj's side and explained, "Arrey Kamat Sir, this boy has a different goal. He has not come here to become a clerk like us. If he manages to secure a position in a marathon, imagine the kind of goodwill that the company will earn. Our brand will get free publicity."

Kamat gave up and said, "You, Rokade sir, have the talent to silence me."

Rokade summoned Lallan Singh and then turned to Kamat saying, "You are senior to me."

Lallan came running in.

"Lallan, take these files and put them back where they had been." Rokade instructed and then continued to appease the devil, "Kamat Sir, let's go get your favorite masala tea. Why do you indulge in these small issues? You should try and stay calm. Come, let's go."

A huge relief washed down Raj.

Consoling him, Monty said, "Don't let your attention get diverted with these frivolous events. Maintain the focus on yourself. Take your seat now and continue your work."

Chapter 26

WHAT GOES AROUND COMES BACK AROUND

After office, Raj put on his running gear and started his run back home. The practice had now become his routine. Every long-distance runner generally faces this problem of time. Since Raj has to be in office from 10 in the morning till 5 in the evening, there was barely any time left for him to practice running. He thus figured out this way to continue his practice, by running to office in the morning hours and running back home in the evening. His formal clothes were taken care of by Monty. He was on his usual run back home, when he crossed the famous Juhu Circle. As his bad fortune would have it, he was spotted by Sam, who was on his bike at the signal, waiting for it to turn green. When it did, he cruised his bike towards Raj and chased him all the way up to the Versova Mosque. As soon as he found a solitary patch, he accelerated the bike and hit Raj with all its force from behind, making him fly off the pavement. Raj screamed in pain, clutching his knee, which was hurt badly. Sam turned his bike around, his tires screeching on the road, and came back towards him.

He took the helmet off of his head to reveal himself and said, "Tit for tat."

He kicked his bike on again and zoomed away. Raj dialled up Monty from his Bluetooth phone and narrated all that had happened with him. Monty reached there with an ambulance in a few minutes and took him to the hospital. Doctor Bamboli took his X-ray and informed to their relief that all his bones were intact.

"Doctor, is he going to be alright soon?" Monty asked concerned.

The Doctor explained, "Actually, his knee joint suffered all the impact. There is certain ligament damage. He should be okay in about 10 to 20 days."

Raj could not believe his words. "What are you saying? It will take 10-20 days to heal?"

"Yes. Ligament injuries take a lot of time."

"Sir, but I have to participate in a marathon which is scheduled for next week."

Dr. Bamboli found himself utterly amused at what he had just heard, "Marathon and you? Now, that is surprising."

Monty elaborated, "Sir, that concept of software change, that you told him about..."

"Yes?"

"He took it very seriously."

"That's really very good for you Raj, but I am so very sorry to inform you that you will not be able to run this marathon. Your knee needs intensive care, which means no movement of the legs. I would suggest that you stay at home and have total rest. The more you rest, the sooner you will recover."

Dr. Bamboli gave the medicines' prescription to Monty while addressing Raj, "Take these medicines twice a day, daily."

CHAPTER 27
DARKNESS EVERYWHERE

Monty supported Raj up their building and took him to his room. Raj's right leg was covered in a brace which restricted all movement. It had become very difficult for him to walk as he couldn't bend his right knee at all. Monty was concerned about Raj's obsession with the marathon. He made Raj lie down comfortably on the bed and asked, "Why is this marathon so important for you? Life is more valuable than running. First, you should focus on getting well. There will be other marathons in the future."

"There is no next time in life," Raj said, looking away.

Monty adopted a stricter tone and said, "Enough with your bullshit motivational phrases. I am more concerned about your health than anything else. Let your injury heal first, then you can go about doing whatever you want."

Raj listened to him quietly.

Monty enquired, "Tell me who did this to you? Who caused this accident?"

"I couldn't see his face."

Raj knew it was Sam, yet he kept quiet.

Monty anger escalated and he said, "You tell me his name. I will break his bones. Bastard." His rage came and went like a huge Tsunami wave, after which he recollected himself and said, "You take rest."

He stood up, switched off the lights and left the room.

Raj closed his eyes and drifted off to sleep.

Raj dreamt of someone drowning. That person was

beating about his arms, trying desperately to reach above the surface, but all his efforts were in vain. It's not that he didn't know how to swim, but somehow his strokes were not sufficient to keep him above the surface of the water. Raj tried hard to see his face, but it was hidden by all the froth and water that was being splashed around. All that he could see were the man's hands and legs flailing about, striving hard to escape. Suddenly, the drowning man's face became visible and Raj woke up in shock. He was thoroughly perturbed to see his own self drowning in water. He was covered in sweat all over and his body was shivering.

Chapter 28

AFTER EVERY NIGHT, THERE IS A DAY

Monty helped Raj reach the beach, the next morning. He then left for his morning jog, leaving Raj seated on a rock. Raj wondered how everything had changed suddenly after the accident. It was the same beach where he had started running initially and now he was rendered utterly incapable of doing it. Raj also felt that while he had lost the chance to run the marathon, he had also lost the opportunity of ever getting Manasi back. His mind was full of questions and there were no answers in sight. Just then Raj saw a boy come running towards him. He recognized him as the boy whom he had seen earlier, the one who was unable to walk and always had a walker beside him. The same boy was now running perfectly fine on his two legs. He noticed Raj too and came to sit on the rock beside him.

Raj asked him anxiously, "Weren't your legs crippled? This is miraculous. When and how did you start running?"

The boy was full of life now and had shed all his past sadness away.

"I just tried. You should also try."

Raj could feel what the boy was trying to tell him. It was better to try than to give up. The boy started reciting a poem which changed his life. Daily, the boy sang the poem loud to Raj.

If you're a diamond
Then become a diamond
If you're a diamond

Then become a diamond
Come out of the coal mine
Remove the blackness from your face
If you want to become a hero
Then do something extraordinary

Water evaporates from the Sun's heat
Then rises above to become a cloud
Comes back to Earth in form of rain
Because it's thirsty for its identity

Struggle is power, know this
Difficulty is a big rock, jump over it
Tears are an ocean, swim through them
Dead man, at least live your life now

If you want to climb a mountain
Then don't be afraid of heights
Believe in yourself and step out

Journey is the destination
Just enjoy the journey
If you want the sky
Then don't be afraid of heights

If you want to become a hero
Then do something extraordinary
If you want to become a hero
Then do something extraordinary

Raj had never expected such motivation to come from a little boy. Aaliya tried to spend as much time with Raj as possible. She prepared his diet plans, gifted him with self-help books, biographies and autobiographies of legends like Haile Gebrselassie and WhatsApp-ed him links to motivational videos on YouTube. The brace on Raj's leg was removed in a day, while it took four more days for the crepe bandage to come off. Starting with brisk walking initially, he soon started running on his legs. However, the confidence to run a full marathon was yet to even touch him.

Aaliya met Raj on Saturday, a day before the marathon. She couldn't contain herself and buried her face in his chest. Hugging him tightly and feeling his arms close around her, she said, "I am so sorry about the marathon. You needn't worry though, you can participate at the Mumbai Marathon next year. It's far more grand than the Pune Marathon."

"For an athlete, only running is grand."

Aaliya turned her head up to look at him and said, "I understand that your mood is off, but destiny has other plans for you."

Raj was surprised to hear that coming from her. "We make our own destiny. It was you who taught me that," he said.

Aaliya looked at this new and transformed Raj wordlessly. This man had changed. She felt as if she had found the man of her dreams - a confident, proud and strong Raj. She was magnetized by his new personality.

"I want to make love to you."

"Aaliya I have some urgent work to do. Please leave me alone."

Aaliya gave him a swift kiss and left.

What could the urgent work for an athlete be, besides preparing for a marathon? Raj really wanted to tell Aaliya that he was planning to run, but kept the urge suppressed inside him.

Raj had started doing his exercises at home using a chair

from the dining table. He got so involved in his routine that day that he didn't hear Monty's footsteps, as he arrived back home from office. Monty was astonished to see what Raj was doing.

"Raj, what is this?" he asked. "The doctor has specifically asked you to take complete rest!"

"Marathon training." Raj answered firmly and decidedly.

"Have you gone mad?"

"This is not madness. This is a need that I have to fulfil."

"What do you gain by putting yourself through so much pain, my friend?"

"I have finally understood myself for the first time. What's the harm in trying?"

"I don't understand your logic or reasoning. You listen to me, I am not letting you go to Pune tomorrow to participate in the marathon. Do you understand?"

Monty stormed out of the room and locked the door behind him. Raj was dumb-founded at his best friend's reaction. We are always betrayed by the closest relations we have in our lives. For Raj, this had happened a second time, after Manasi.

CHAPTER 29

THE MOTH BECAME A CATERPILLAR

It was 5 A.M. when Monty woke up from sleep. He felt the need to go check on Raj so he unlocked the door of his room and entered. Raj was not on his bed. He checked the washroom, he was not there either. He could see some books scattered on Raj's bed from which he understood that Raj must have left for Pune to participate in the marathon. Pune was only two hours from Mumbai and Raj didn't face any traffic at night. He reached the venue well before time.

It was the 29th Pune International Marathon (PIM), which was one of India's most premium Marathon events. Since 1983, thousands of runners from all walks of life had been taking part in it. It had come to be used widely as a platform for spreading social messages and raising funds for charitable cause. The route winded through Pune's most scenic and historic locations, while thousands of spectators lined up the course to cheers the runners on. It was the most anticipated running festival for the city of Pune. Every registered participant was given a T-Shirt, Certificate, Medal and Time Chips. The event attracted almost over 40,000 participants from India and 35 other countries from around the world every year. With approximately 15 lakh runners having participated in it till then, it boasted of hosting eminent personalities like Late Rajiv Gandhi, Milkha Singh, PT Usha, Kapil Dev, Leander Peas & many others who participated in the run. The highest record in men's category was held by Kenya's Joseph Kahugu with a time of 2hrs : 13mins : 00secs in 1996, and in women's category by Ethiopia's Birzah Tekele with a time of 2hrs : 38mins : 41secs in 2010.

PIM was recognized as a national championship as well as an international event where Indian athletes brushed shoulders with leading International marathoners. The said event had given a major boost to the country's long distance runners, many of whom were from Maharashtra and went on to win medals at Common Wealth and Asian Games.

All the runners gathered at the starting point. 189 runners from outside India were put in the Elite Athletes category and were given the front position, immediately followed by the top Indian runners. Doordarshan, along with a local cable channel, had set up arrangements for a live telecast. A commentary was already underway by the international marathoner Chris Baun and the Indian international marathoner, Sardar Singh. A big LED screen at the starting point displayed a live telecast of the event. The cameramen were ready on bikes, open air jeeps and cars. TV reporters from India and abroad were speaking into their cameras, reporting the events of the morning.

The big screen displayed pictures of Dennis Kipruto Kimetto from Kenya, who held the World's top position in Men's Marathon with a record breaking time of 2 hours, 2 minutes and 57 seconds at the 2014 Berlin Marathon. His profile was followed by other Elite Athletes from Kenya, Ethiopia, Uganda and other countries, following which the Indian Athletes came.

Raj saw his own profile on the big screen. He was surrounded by other top Indian athletes at the starting line. He had no expectations from himself. He had only gone there to try. Even finishing the 42.195 kilometers was not his ambition.

The prize money for the marathon's champion was

declared Rs. 2.5 lacs, which meant a lot for the athletes from African countries. Few Ethiopian athletes shook hands with each other and it appeared as if they were the probable winners. One of those athletes looked terribly concerned and distant from the rest of them. He got a phone call just then, and walked over to the Indian athletes' area to pick it up. He was standing right next to Raj when he picked up the call. A little girl's voice came from the other end, and tears start to roll down his eyes. The little girl on the other end was his daughter. Raj glanced at his chest plate which stated that he was Titoss from Ethiopia. His tears drew Raj's concern and he tried to understand the reason behind Titoss' anguish by his tone and the dispersed words of English in his conversation. He figured that somebody back home in Ethiopia desperately needed money. Raj's interest in the conversation escalated and he heard the daughter speak the final sentence,

"If you fail to bring money, mother will die in the hospital."

Titoss walked back to his allotted section and the sound of the live commentary grew louder.

Sardar Singh preached, "Chris, I once asked a marathoner, 'Why do you run?' Do you know what he replied? 'I run marathons to forget myself. My mind becomes dead while I am running.'"

Chris cheered on, "All athletes, get ready for the great marathon!"

A voice boomed from the loudspeaker, "The countdown begins, 3....2.....1....go!"

The hooter blew and the chief guest flagged off the event.

The Pune International Marathon had officially started. A large and enthusiastic crowd had gathered all through the route to cheer on thousands of people who were running the distance of 42.195 kilometers. Such international marathons had always been dominated by Kenyans and Ethiopians;

never had an Indian ever won an International Marathon like it.

African athletes followed the strategy of smart intensive running and had set a good pace already. The genetic buildup, lifestyle and geographical terrain that the Africans live with, has a contributing role to play in making them the world's fasters runners and the most enduring athletes.

The big screen now displayed the World Record split of 2014 Berlin Marathon, where Dennis Kimetto covered the first 10 kilometers in 29 minutes and 24 seconds.

Chris narrated, "You can see the amount of effort these International athletes are putting in."

Sardar Singh added, "Marathon is much like our own life. It's not about the number of obstacle we face, but how we face those obstacles, how we fight them. No matter whether you run slow or swift, once you cross the finishing line, your life changes forever."

Indian runners were performing at their best speed too. Ram Singh lead the pack of Indian runners. Raj was in this group as well.

The receptionist, back at Raj's gym in Mumbai, was busy with her usual routine when his name attracted her attention to the running commentary of the marathon on TV. She leaned forward across her desk to look at the television screen more closely. As soon as she saw Raj on the live feed, running amongst the top runners of the nation, she was ecstatic. She immediately rushed to the gym area to share the news with fellow gym members.

She exclaimed, almost shouting, "Guys! Our Raj is running at the marathon on T.V. Come on!"

Everyone dropped their exercise equipment and rushed towards the T.V. to watch their new hero, Raj.

A boy in a white shirt cheered loudly, "Come on! Come

on! Come on, Raj!"

Another boy in a bundy exclaimed, "This is Raj, yaar! Raj!"

A girl shouted, "This is Raj! Wow....great. This is incredible."

The receptionist rushed on to the cycling room.

Sam, Santosh and Vigyan were exercising there.

Santosh was angry with Sam and said, "Sam you did wrong, it was not fair."

"This was my reply to Aaliya's knock. She should have thought twice before hitting me," Sam said arrogantly.

The receptionist entered the cycling area just then. "Guys! Our Raj is leading the Marathon. Come on!" she exclaimed excitedly.

Santosh made a sarcastic remark as soon as she left, "He has hit back, and so much harder this time."

Sam could not believe his ears and followed the receptionist to confirm for himself, while the others followed him.

A boy pointed his finger at the screen and yelled, "Look, that's our Raj!"

Another girl cheered on, "Come on, woohoo!"

All the gym members, along with the receptionist, cooed and celebrated with chants of "We love you Raj."

Commentator Chris's voice cut through the cheers at the gym, "Raj has left the Indians' pack behind."

Sam couldn't believe that Raj had managed to recover from the massive accident so quickly.

Back at Raj and Monty's office, everyone had come in the first shift on Sunday to finish the pending work alloted by Mr. Kamat, the dictator. Suddenly the peon, Lallan Singh, rushed out of the conference room.

He called out excitedly to everyone present there, "Arey

Kamat saheb, Rokade sir, Kamini madam, arey Gupta ji, Verma ji!"

Everyone was quick to attention. Lallan Singh never dared to speak in a loud voice at office but he couldn't contain himself that day.

Kamini responded to him first. "What happened?"

He announced loudly, "Everyone, listen carefully. Our Raj Sir is running the International Marathon in Pune."

Kamat could not believe his ears, "Are we foolish enough to believe that?"

Rokade jumped from his seat and rushed towards the conference room. The others followed him.

Kamat was displeased with the indiscipline in office but the tide was not in his favour that day.

Everyone started cheering for Raj in the conference room. The huge screen on one wall displayed the live telecast of the marathon.

"Running very fast," Mishra ji commented.

Srivastava said praising, "Our Raj is running like a bullet train."

Mishra ji contradicted him in fun, "You liar, he is faster than that."

Chris continues with his commentary, "Raj is pacing up and has reached the pack of Elite Athletes now."

Kamat entered the conference room to witness the electricity in the air that the great event had brought on.

Rokade mocked at Kamat saying, "Kamat sir, I feel that he is able to run so fast because of the fear of you."

Kamat kept looking awkwardly at the T.V. screen where Raj was slowly crossing past all the African runners.

Sardar Singh exclaimed from the commentator's box, "My eyes have waited so long for this moment!"

Aaliya had been sleeping in her room. Her mother

brought in a cup of herbal tea for her. Aaliya woke up and heard the sound of commentary coming from the other room. She remembered that it was the day of the marathon. The very next moment however, she recalled that Raj was not participating in it and closed her eyes again.

"Your friend Raj is running at the marathon," her mother told her.

Aaliya jumped up in surprise and said, "My God! Unbelievable."

Aaliya rushed to the other room, her eyes wide open. "How is he here?" she wondered.

Her father was reading the newspaper in front of the T.V. "He is the first Indian to run at this speed," he said.

Aaliya felt proud of Raj. She couldn't believe that he was running at such speed inspite of his knee injury.

Meanwhile at the gym, everyone that had gathered around the T.V. screen were having a blast, chanting and celebrating Raj's excellent performance. The working staff, the chaiwala, the cleaner and the watchman had also flocked in to see what the commotion was about.

The entire city echoed with the sound of cheering for Raj. Within a few moments, he went from being a nobody to a household name. People all over the world had their eyes set on Raj.

Remembering Raj's early days at the gym, a member commented, "This is the same guy whose stomach used to ache whenever he ran."

A boy in a blue t-shirt added, "I can't believe my eyes. He use to run on the treadmill here and now he is running at marathon and leading it too. Come on Raj…come on!"

The gym manager entered the area and said, "Unbelievable! We have a champion runner from our gym…Come on Raj!"

Monty was browsing through T.V. channels when

suddenly he saw Raj's name feature in the headline of a News channel. They were calling Raj the latest sensation in the sports industry.

Monty repented his mistake in stopping Raj and cheered on, "Run, my tiger…my cheetah…run!"

Manasi was at a supermarket purchasing groceries when a television screen on the wall caught her attention. All the sets at the electronics section of the store were displaying the live marathon in Pune. She was astounded by what she saw. Raj, her husband, was leading the marathon. Not even in her wildest dreams had she imagined him to be running this way. She knew Raj as a man who could barely jog a mile, and now he was leading a full marathon. It was utterly amazing and unbelievable for her.

Raj was running at his top speed and managed to leave all the International athletes behind. His mind began to wander off to memories from his past. Bad reminiscences started to flash across his mind one after the other.

He was transported back to the vegetable market with Manasi. "This man understands nothing. Forget it," he heard her say.

He then saw her confronting him after the thief stole her mangalsutra. "I don't want to talk to you."

Manasi's voice filled his head. "Stupid loser. I hate him, I hate him, I hate him. What will people say? Loser's wife. Loser's wife. Loser's wife. You are a confused person, confused, confused. The day you become a hero from zero, I will come back to you myself."

Kamat's words started ringing in his ears too. "The energy he puts into running, had he put the same in his work, he would have reached great heights by now."

Raj eliminated these thoughts from his head as he knew they would do him no good. They only served to demotivate him and put him down in his own eyes. He knew and believed this time that one becomes that what one thinks of oneself. Seeding the correct thought in mind was the primary task towards achieving a goal. Raj turned his thoughts around to focus on all the positivity and inspiration that he had gathered in the past few months.

First, he thought of his interaction with Doctor Bamboli. "Delete the thought from your mind that your stomach aches when you run. Instead, load a new software which tells you that you can run."

As soon as the thought spread through his mind, a smile rose automatically on his face.

He recollected all the positive motivation that Aaliya had given him. "You run 21 kilometers so easily. I guarantee, you can definitely win the 42 kilometers marathon too."

He remembered the affirmation session with Aaliya at Matherun. "I am the best…I am the best…I am the best." He started feeling great again.

Since, Raj was already far ahead of his competitors, he felt confident that the Pune International Marathon was in his hands. However, this slight streak of over-confidence inflated his ego and blinded him. Raj lost his view of the road and stepped over a small stone lying in his way. The calf muscle of his right leg got pulled and his body was thrown to one side. He cried out in pain and the cameramen zoomed in on him from all sides. None came to his aid.

"India's luck in sports faces yet another thrashing. An Indian who seemed like he was going to be the first ever champion of an International marathon, lies flat on the ground," the commentator stated.

Meanwhile, Aaliya, Manasi, Monty, the office colleagues, the gym members and the rest of the world watched him with bated breaths. Aaliya immediately ran to her bedroom to look for her phone. She knew that Raj always carried a small phone connected to Bluetooth with him. She came back and dialled his number, her eyes fixed on the T.V. screen. Raj heard the phone ringing and immediately guessed it to be Aaliya. He pressed the receiving button on his Bluetooth device and heard her voice from the other side.

"I can see you on T.V., what happened exactly?" she asked worried.

"Calf Muscle got pulled," Raj managed to speak through the pain, his teeth clenched tight.

"Don't worry, don't worry. Just relax!" she said, trying to calm him down.

Raj massages his calf muscle and let it set in slowly. He followed her words and tried to relax his mind. He fought off the thoughts of not winning and worse, of not even being able to finish the marathon. The elite group of International runners crossed him.

Regardless, he concentrated on Aaliya's directions. "Do what I say. Raise your left leg to 10 degrees."

Raj lifted the leg and his calf muscle set down properly to it's original place. He felt indescribable pain as he did it.

Aaliya continues, "Now 45 degrees…yes…very good… now 90 degrees…yes, correct, good…How you are feeling now?"

Raj felt a little relaxed. Seeking the opportunity, Aaliya urged him on to stand up. Right behind him, the top group of Indian runners was approaching.

Raj balanced himself on his legs and tried to walk forward. Aaliya asked him to aim the next red light as the finishing point and walk faster. Raj experienced sharp waves of pain shooting through his legs but kept walking. The Indian group passed him by.

Aaliya instructed, "Now try to jog a bit."

Raj managed that perfectly well.

"Raj, I am going to hypnotize you for a while now." Aaliya confessed in a serious tone.

"Why?"

"To remove the blockage in your mind that you are injured."

"Will that work?"

"Do you want to win?"

"From my heart and soul."

"Then surrender your mind to me."

"I am surrendering my mind to you."

"Raj, your leg is perfectly fine. Believe that you are alright. Know that you are the only one who can win this marathon. Remember all the effort you put in mountain training, sand training, Chi training and all other forms of training. This is the moment that you've lived for. You have to run and run faster than you have ever run before."

Those words were more than enough to motivate Raj into running faster.

"Can you tell me how far the Indian group is?" Raj asked her.

Aaliya waited for the stats to be displayed on the T.V. and found out that the Indian group was about 500 meters ahead of Raj and they had already covered a distance of 32 kilometers. Aaliya then quickly grabbed a pen and paper and started doing the arithmetic to calculate the speed Raj needed to reach the Indian group.

Aaliya summarized, "You need to accelerate and cover the next kilometer in lesser time, that is the only way that you can catch up to them in the next two kilometers."

Raj did as she instructed. He kept repeating to himself, "I am a champion, I am a winner."

After the mantra which Aaliya gave Raj feels fresher than

he was before. His body had accepted the command that was given to it. His brain was under control like a perfect servant and his soul ruled over his heart and mind. Raj did the extra ordinary and reached the pack of Indian athletes.

A ray of hope shone through for the television viewers. Manasi couldn't believe what she was witnessing. The office conference room was electric with all the enthusiasm and Kamat came into a different form unknown to everyone till then. He hollered like a child, "Come on Raj! You can do it." At the gym, all the members continued to cheer for Raj. Even Sam started to feel for him.

A single event had changed everyone's perspective towards him. Raj's destination was yet out of reach for him. However, with a guardian angel like Aaliya, Raj felt like he could achieve anything.

Aaliya checked the distance between Raj and the International Athletes.

"Raj, you only need to cover a total distance of seven kilometers now."

"Seven. How far are they?"

"Far enough."

Aaliya tallied the average speeds of the top runners over the Internet and matched it with their speeds in the last kilometer.

"As per the record, Titoss has a higher ranking than anyone else here. But he has a tendency to lose out in the last kilometer. He will start to accelerate after two kilometers. Rest of the runners should finish the marathon behind him for sure."

"What speed should I aim for?"

"Five minutes per mile."

"I have never run at that pace before."

"It doesn't mean that you cannot do it now," she said

motivating him.

"I affirm that."

"Feel as if you are Dennis Kimetto himself. Do what he did at the Berlin Marathon."

"Are you asking me to feel like the World's fastest marathoner?"

"I am asking you to become a little better than him. I am asking you to run at 4.4 minutes per mile."

"If there is no way, then I will do it."

When life gives you no options, it is a definite sign that you are going to make it. Raj was sprinting as he had never done before. To run at such a pace at his first marathon, that too after a massive calf muscle injury was beyond belief. Raj caught on with the group 3 kilometers before the finish line. Five athletes had maintained a lead at various distances ahead, with Titoss in the first position.

Aaliya was multi-tasking with the paper and pen, her mobile, the television and the internet on her laptop.

"Raj, it seems impossible to defeat Titoss."

"Let me catch up with the four running ahead first."

Raj remembered the training that Samantha had given her, of stretching the strides in the last few kilometres to cover more ground. All the instructions that his trainers had given him and all the books which he had read, were now flashing across his mind. Raj passed by two African athletes easily, and was left with just three in front of him. The competition between India, Kenya and Ethiopia was on. People from all across the globe were glued to their television sets, watching the incredible competition. Raj had not only become a national hero, but was also an international star now.

"You only have three more runners to defeat. Keep your focus on Titoss and run as if you have only him to defeat.

You're one kilometer away from the finish line now."

The others two athletes started to accelerate too. Raj crossed the third athlete and attained the third position for himself. Many Indian athletes had previously finished third and it was a great achievement in itself, but Raj was not satisfied with it. Two separate minds were working parallel-y for Raj; one, his own and other, that of Aaliya. At that moment, he was two people in one. As forecasted by Aaliya, Titoss had started to lose his speed. He looked back to check his position; he was only 30 meters ahead of the second runner. Raj was about to cross the athlete in the second position, who was full of rage as he had not expected an Indian to get ahead of him. He did not allow Raj to cross and kept blocking his way. Aaliya thought of an idea.

"Run right behind him for a while and when I give the command, leap ahead of him in a flash," she suggested.

Aaliya waited for the perfect opportunity. The moment she saw a wide gap on the left side of the road, she exclaimed into the phone, "Cross him from the left side, now!" Raj quickly leaped ahead of him.

Monty's eyes were brimming with tears. Rokade could not contain himself and went out of the conference room. Manasi felt emotionally robbed. The gymnasium was buzzing as if a festival was on. The gym manager announced a lifetime's free membership for Raj. The CEO at Raj's company gave him an instant promotion. The state government announced a Pradesh Ratna Award for him. But his task was yet unfinished.

"Raj, you are on your own now. Remember, NOW or NEVER!" Aaliya said and disconnected the call.

Her mother asked, "Why did you disconnect the call when he needed you the most?"

Aaliya replied, "I want him to own his victory."

"Do you love him?" she asked her.

"Yes mom," she said smiling.

Her father was listening to their conversation carefully. "Will he marry you?" he asked.

"No," Aaliya replied.

Both her parents looked at each other but said nothing.

The whole country was at the edge of their seats. All the media had gathered to record the historic footage first hand. Raj was still ten meters behind Titoss, while only two hundred meters remained before the finish line. People gathered on either side of the road cheered him on. The volunteers were finding it exceedingly difficult to tame the roaring spectators. Children stood with handmade banners with messages such as 'Raj is a Hero', 'I love you', 'Best of the best' etc., written on them.

Raj kept repeating to himself, "I will do it."

Meanwhile, Titoss was out of breath and his strides grew shorter and slower. Raj was gaining speed and soon reached parallel to him. A stream of tears were flowing down Aaliya's cheeks. She knew his Raj has won over himself. Raj and Titoss had a good view of each other. Raj could see the frustration on his face, but nothing was going to stop him. He crossed Titoss when the last 50 meters were left to cover. As he approached the finishing line, he felt complete silence, not outside but inside his head. He could not hear or feel or sense anything at all. He felt as if he had dissolved into complete consciousness. He was absolutely detached from the external world. In this new-found world, only he existed; no body, no mind, no heart, but a pure consciousness.

After a moment, something flashed through his mind, the vision of Titoss talking to his daughter. He looked back. Titoss was exerting all his energy towards the finishing line, but somewhere deep inside him he had come to realise that he had lost the battle and his wife.

Suddenly, the entire crowd became silent. Jaws dropped and all the applause and cheering stopped. The media was shocked too. Aaliya couldn't believe what was happening and hugged her mother tight. Kamat's mouth was wide open, while Monty was taken back. Raj had stopped about a meter before the finishing line. Everyone screamed and yelled for him to cross the line but Raj stayed unmoving. Titoss arrived at the spot in seconds and Raj gestured at him to cross the line ahead of him. Tears bursted through Titoss' eyes. He stopped and gave Raj a hug. He offered Raj his hand which he took and they crossed the finishing line together. Raj however, made sure that Titoss step the line first. He became the winner, while Raj came in second.

Titoss hugged him again and said, "Thank you. You saved my wife."

Raj smiled at him and said, "The prize money was never my aim. I just wanted to win, win over myself."

"You have won the hearts of people all over the world," Titoss replied with a wide grin.

The media personnel came running towards Titoss as he was the new champion and the event organizers escorted him away for live interviews. Raj turned his head up to look at the sky and thanked the universe.

The very next moment he reached for his phone and made a call. Aaliya picked up at the other end.

"Aaliya, can you meet me in the evening?"

"Yes."

Before Aaliya could say another word, he disconnected the call.

Raj arrived back home where Monty was waiting to welcome him. He congratulated his friend and left for an evening shift at office. Raj went straight to his bathroom and turned on the shower. The cool drops of water on his face felt like a blessing from God. His entire body was drained out.

The fatigue had finally started to roll in with full force and he could barely stand. He sat on the floor under the shower for almost an hour, after which he made his way back to the bedroom. He didn't realise when he drifted off to sleep, but when he woke up, he found Aaliya right beside him. She was looking at him with adoring eyes, filled with all the love that she felt for him. The very next moment he realized that he was completely nude. He tried to put the towel onto him and Aaliya smiled at his frantic effort. Raj looked at her and said, "I want to say something to you."

"I am listening," she said beaming.

"Can you give me energy?"

Aaliya understood what he wanted. She started to undo the buttons on her denim jacket. Raj stopped her and Aaliya turned her face up to look at him, surprised.

Raj looked deep into her eyes and said, "I want to undress you today."

Aaliya couldn't believe his words. She resigned herself completely to him. Raj undressed her slowly. Both of them took a moment to look at each other, after which Aaliya surrendered and let Raj dominate. He lunged forward to kiss her and she responded with pleasure. She felt that Raj was different and more passionate this time. Aaliya let herself get carried away with the flow. Raj supported himself on top of her and asked, "Can I?"

Aaliya nodded with tears in her eyes. She felt pure ecstasy as Raj slowly entered her.

With each successive thrust, he said,

"I"

"Love"

"You"

Aaliya's unconditional love had won the heart of her man. Thereafter, they made love the entire night and became one.

Chapter 30

CATERPILLAR IS NOW A BUTTERFLY

Back from the haze of his memories, Raj found himself standing tall at the seaside again, waiting for someone. He folded the letter and placed it back in his pocket. Jumping down from the pipe structure, he walked over to another point to have a better view of the sea. Raj, who had barely been a drop of water till a few months past, had fought ahead to join a stream, became a river and ultimately managed to join the ocean. His journey had been both enriching as well as fulfilling. A woman wearing a red saree looked at him from a distance and started walking towards him. The reader might guess it to be Aaliya, but it wasn't her. It was Manasi, the cherry on the cake that Raj had been craving all this while. He was, however, unaware of her presence there. When Manasi reached up close to him and saw him lost in his thoughts, she could not stop herself from hugging him. Raj recovered from his thoughts and found her in his arms, the woman that he had always pined for. The one for whom he had done it all was right there in his arms. Manasi hugged him so tight that her nails dug into his back.

She said, "I am sorry Raj. I want to come back to you."

Raj pulled away from her embrace and undid her arms from around him.

He replied, "Thank you Manasi. If you hadn't left me, I would never have understood myself. I had forgotten that all of us come to this world alone and leave it alone likewise. Why then should we waste our lives away for the love of another? Why not love ourselves?"

"But you always wanted me," Manasi urged.

"Not anymore."

Manasi understood his tone and did not say a word more.

"Manasi, I have to go for practice." Raj said and turned around. He started to move away, while Manasi watched him leave.

After a moment, she yelled after him, "Raj."

Raj turned to look at her as she said, "You are a hero. All the best."

Raj smiled at her and replied, "Thank you."

After running for about a mile, he received a call from Aaliya.

"Where are you, lover boy?" she asked.

Raj chuckled and said, "Coming to you."

"To me?"

"Yes, I wanted to ask something important from you."

"What is it?" she asked giggling.

"Where would you like to go for our honeymoon?" he asked without any hint of hesitation.

Aaliya couldn't believe what she was hearing. "Are you proposing to me?" she asked.

"Yes."

Aaliya jumped with joy but came to herself the very next moment.

"But you are still married," she stated, confused.

Raj said assuringly, "I am filing for divorce tomorrow."

"I am so lucky to have you," Aaliya said, thanking him.

Raj dismissed her saying, "No, I am lucky to have you."

Both of them shared a warm laugh.

"You didn't tell me. Where should we go for our honeymoon?" he asked again.

"The place where your ultra-marathon is going to be

held,' she replied cheerfully.

"South Africa?"

"Of course, South Africa!"

"I have to run the Comrades Marathon, but what will you do there?"

"Teach you the two hundred and forty-five kamasutra positions."

Raj laughed out loud and Aaliya joined him.

Raj married Aaliya, soon after his divorce with Manasi was finalized. Both of them participated in marathons together all over the world.

The End

'Jeet Lo Marathon' the motion picture has been made under the banner of Soulandhearts Films and will be releasing soon. Please watch the film in theatres near you.

The Cast of the movie is as follows:

Aryan	Raj
Ankita Bahuguna	Manasi
Preena Jhamb	Aaliya
Anjani Kumar Singh	Monty
Retd. W. C. Rajiv Khare	Rokade
Chandre Meiring	Samantha
Abhishek Soti	Ram Singh
Shashi Bhushan Tiwari	Lallan Singh
Gautam Berde	Dr. Bamboli
Jitendra Kumar Jaiswal	Kamat
C P Bhatt	Shopkeeper
Sawan Kumar Shukla	Thief
Sangeeta Bhosle	Manasi's Mom
Vishal Dudhavade	CEO
Farah	Kamini
Ganesh More	Sam
Kishore Kulkarni	Aaliya's Father
Premakiran	Aaliya's Mom

Our sincere gratitude to
All the sportsmen around the world.

Team Jeet Lo Marathon Movie

Sri Hitendra Thakur, Dr. Gauri Chaudhary, Dr.Sandeep Kante, Kaizzad Kapadia, Staff of 5 fitness gymnasiums and K11 academy, residents of Ruia Park Apartment, Juhu, Mumbai Police, Viva Electronics Virar, Sanjeev Ratan, Arya Pandey, Pradipto Nandi, Mushtaq Pasa, Vikas Kapoor, Creative Eye Productions, Gaurav, Avneesh, Kamal, Manoj Adhikari, Sanjay Adhikari, Stance Productions, N P Singh, Rahul, Kaushik of Le Doors Productions, Barun Mukherjee, Girish, Dipali Majithia, Sanjay (Vikalp, New Delhi).

Teachers and cadets of U P Sainik School, Lucknow, teachers and staff of St. Mary Convent School, Ghazipur and Dakpather, Mini Montessori School, SFFSS School Herbertpur, Saraswati Shishu Vidya Mandir Ballia, Lucknow University, Ved Bhardwaj, Sunita Bhardwaj, Pankaj B Singh, Preenal Oberoi Singh, Pradeep Kumar Rai, Sameer Bhatnagar & family, Lt. Col Brijesh Gautam, Vikram Prasad and family, Subir Das.

Vivek Shah, Meeta Shah and family, Anil Jain, Shubha Durwar, Shyam Bhardwaj and family, Parimal, Shalini Mishra, Abhay Kumar Mishra, Ruchi Tiwari, Tanuja Bajpai, Cricket Team Lucknow, Sudhanshu Srivastava and family, Amit Sharma and family, Y P Singh, Amrit Lal, Reshma Rathod Madam, Deepti madam, Maria madam, Arvind Bachel Sir, A R Gentyela Sir, S Gairola Sir, Rajneesh, Vinoda Madam, Ritu Madam, Shinde Sir, Shobha Madam, Luana Madam, Dipali Madam, Veena Madam, Kalyani Madam, Pradyna Madam, Pravin Joshi sir, Sahare sir, Bhagyashree Madam, Prafull, Vasudev Kamat, B V Chaubal, Shiv Kumar, K C Agarwal, P C Pandey, Batch SBI PO 2001, Abhay Mishra, Rashmi Mishra, Ruchi Tiwari, Tanuja Chaturvedi, Anurag Sir, Amit

Sir, Himanshu Sir, Neeraj Pant, Shikhar Srivastava, Bareilly Cricket Team, Lucknow Cricket Team, Abhilasha and family. Dharmvardhan and family, Meet, Buddy's of Indirapuram, Subhash Joshi, James Lyall, Navender, Ashish Arya, P C Kushwaha, Marathon Baba, Krishna Rai, Vikas Soni, Selva Selva Selva.

Kul Devi of our family, Mirzapur family, Varanasi family, Lucknow family, Guria didi, Jijaji, Charu and her brother, Prince and family, Amit, Gaurav, Nanaji and Naniji, Sanjay Mama and Shail Mamiji, Pinki Mausi, Poonam Mausi, Usha Mausi, Pankaj Bhaiya and family, Biharilal Fufaji, Kamal Bhaiya and family, Santosh Chahaji and family, Sunita chahi, Neeshu, Neetu and Putul chachaji, Azzo Chachaji and family, Kamal Chachaji and family, Chanda Buwa and family.

Citizens of Lucknow, Thane, Satara, Matheran, Pune, Virar and Mauritius.

Events viz. Minithon by Spic, Mira Bhayendar Marathon, Rutu Kalyan Marathon, Valsad City Half Marathon, Meditation Run Pune, Chalo Sath Chale Pune, Faridabad Marathon, Thrill Zone New Delhi Half Marathon, Thrill Zone Mumbai Half Marathon, Thrill Zone Chandigarh Promo Run, Surat Cricket Tournament, Highway Runners, Chembur Mini Marathon, Kolkata Half Marathon, Borivali Walkathon, Champios Club 21 K, Road Show at Nariman Point, Runners Academy Night, Brahamakumari Festival Borivali, Matunga ICT Marathon, Charkhop Marathon, Sattva Fest by Mukesh Patel School of Technology, management and commerce, ajit pathak of pinkathon runners, P. C. Kushwaha, Vivek Soni, Sudarshan K Singh, Nanda Shetty, Manjay Yadav, Hetal Kevat Gym Valsad, Nilesh Valsad, Noida Half Marathon,Neeru Bajaj, Mayank Singh, Rajan Luthra, Sachin Sagar, Jeet Lo Marathon participants.

Win Marathon

Be a Hero

References:

1. Meditation – Wikipedia
2. Mauritius- Wikipedia
3.Chi running – Internet
4. Pune International Marathon – Official website
5. Cast – Jeet Lo Marathon Website (http://www.marathonthefilm.in)
6. Soundtrack of the film can be found on the YouTube Channel of Soulandhearts Film
7. Facebook Page of Jeet Lo Marathon: https://www.facebook.com/jeetlomarathon
8. Aryan blogs at aryanvisionary.blogspot.com
9. Aryan's personal YouTube page: YouTube/aryanavisionary
10. Instagram/neerrajanand and JeetLo_Marathon
11. Twitter/neerrajanand and JeetLo_Marathon
12. Imdb/WinMarathon